Ellen gasped. Her hands flew to her mouth and she stepped backward.

Two transparent hands floated up from inside the large black urn that was the oldest piece of Wedgwood in the Clayton collection. They were a woman's hands with tapered fingernails and they looked absolutely real, except that Ellen could see right through them.

Slowly the hands drifted toward Ellen. The fingers were outstretched, the way the hands of the woman in the mirror had been, as if the owner of the hands were begging.

Ellen took another step backward. The hands followed. They floated toward her, the fingers rippling slowly . . .

Ellen tried to speak, to tell the hands to go away, but her mouth felt glued shut. She felt like a statue, fastened in concrete to that spot in the floor, unable to move or speak . . . .

Books by Peg Kehret

Cages
Horror at the Haunted House
Nightmare Mountain
Sisters, Long Ago
Terror at the Zoo

Available from MINSTREL Books

Horror at the Haunted House

PEG KEHRET

A MINSTREL JR BOOK

PUBLISHED BY POCKET BOOKS

New York   London   Toronto   Sydney   Tokyo   Singapore

This book is a work of fiction. Names, characters, places
and incidents are products of the author's imagination or are
used fictitiously. Any resemblance to actual events or locales
or persons, living or dead, is entirely coincidental.

A Minstrel Book published by
POCKET BOOKS, a division of Simon & Schuster Inc.
1230 Avenue of the Americas, New York, NY 10020

Copyright © 1992 by Peg Kehret

Published by arrangement with Cobblehill Books,
an affiliate of Dutton Children's Books,
a division of Penguin Books USA Inc.

ISBN: 0-671-86685-0

First Minstrel Books printing November 1994

10 9 8 7 6 5 4 3 2 1

A MINSTREL BOOK and colophon are registered
trademarks of Simon & Schuster Inc.

Cover art by Danilo Ducak

Printed in the U.S.A.

FOR BRETT MICHELLE

OCTOBER 31, 1989

Special thanks to
Myra Karp of Wedgwood World, Seattle,
and to Daisy Makeig-Jones

Chapter
1

Hey, Ellen! I'm going to have my head chopped off!"

Over the din on the school bus, Ellen Streater recognized her younger brother's voice. She peered through the window. Corey waved and ran along the sidewalk.

Ellen's best friend, Caitlin, nudged Ellen with her elbow and muttered, "I'm glad he's your brother, not mine."

As the yellow bus wheezed to a stop, Corey yelled again. "I'm going to have my head chopped off!"

Ellen was used to her brother's fanciful stories but she wished he would wait until she got home. As she stepped off the bus, she heard her classmates snickering.

Corey danced with excitement. "It's going to happen in a haunted house," he said. "Mr. Teen is going to chop my head off with a big knife."

The bus rumbled away. Ellen started down the sidewalk toward home with Corey bouncing beside her. "You sound awfully happy for someone who's about to be murdered," she said.

Corey giggled. "I won't *really* get my head chopped off," he said, "but it will look like I do. There's a big wooden contraption with a rope and a fat sharp knife and Mr. Teen wears a black hood with only his eyes showing. I get to put my head on a wooden block and then Mr. Teen lets go of the rope and all the people watching will think the knife cut off my head. There's even going to be fake blood."

"Exactly who is this Mr. Teen?" Ellen said.

"He's Grandma's friend. She told me all about it."

Ellen raised her eyebrows. Grandma's friend? Corey's stories ordinarily did not include real people. Was he telling the truth, for a change? Or at least his garbled version of the truth?

"Are you making up a story?" she said.

"No! Grandma fixed it so we could get killed in the haunted house."

Ellen stopped walking. "WE?" she said. "Am I supposed to get my head chopped off, too?"

"Oh, no," Corey said. "You get tied up and burned at the stake."

"I can hardly wait."

Ellen saw her grandmother's car parked in the Streaters' driveway. She hurried inside, gave Grandma a quick hug, and said, "Would you please tell me what's going on?"

"How would you like to participate in a Halloween haunted house?" Grandma said.

"That depends on whether I come out of it dead or alive."

Grandma laughed. "I don't think Mrs. Whittacker would ask you to do anything dangerous."

Mrs. Whittacker was Grandma's best friend. She had no grandchildren of her own so she frequently baked cookies for

Ellen and Corey and always gave them a small gift on their birthdays.

"Mrs. Whittacker is President of the Historical Society and her group is renovating Clayton House, the mansion that was donated to the city. It's a gorgeous old house and Mr. Clayton also donated the furnishings. There are antique music boxes, hand-carved tables and chairs, an extensive collection of Wedgwood, stained-glass lampshades—I could go on and on. The Historical Society plans to turn the mansion into a museum, with the Clayton treasures on display, but they need funds in order to get the house ready for public viewing."

"So they're making it into a haunted house," said Corey. "And we get to be in it. We'll be famous! Maybe we'll get our picture in the paper."

"It's being called the Historical Haunted House," Grandma said. "Each room will be a horrible scene from history, and people will pay to take the tour. Many local celebrities are donating their time to act as characters in the scenes. They'll reenact the duel between Alexander Hamilton and Aaron Burr in 1804 and the stabbing of Julius Caesar and . . ."

"Who were they?" said Corey.

"You'll need to find that out," said Grandma, "if you want to enter the prize drawing. All of the scenes except one will be historically accurate. When people finish viewing the haunted house, they can write down which scene is not based on fact and all the correct answers will be entered in a drawing. The prize is one hundred dollars. There will be twenty scenes in all—even a medieval torture chamber."

"Are you sure Mom and Dad will let us do this?" asked Ellen. A stabbing and a torture chamber did not sound like the sort of event her parents would normally approve of.

3

"I called your mother," Grandma replied, "and she said it is OK with her if you want to help, since the scenes *are* authentic. You'll get a history lesson and the money is for a good cause."

"Tell her about my part," Corey said. "Tell her about me getting my head chopped off."

"Corey will be Prince Rufus, who was beheaded at the age of ten," Grandma said.

"I get to scream," Corey said. "Loud." His eyes sparkled. "Tell her about Mr. Teen," he said.

"Who?" said Grandma.

"Mr. Teen. The one who's going to wear a black hood and chop off my head."

Grandma looked confused for a moment and then started to laugh. "Not Mr. Teen," she said. "Guillotine. That's the name of the instrument with the knife. The man in the black hood will be Mike McGarven."

"Mighty Mike?" said Corey. "The D.J.?"

Grandma nodded.

"Wow," said Corey. "I'm going to meet Mighty Mike. Wait till Nicholas hears this." He picked up the telephone and began punching his friend's number.

Ellen didn't blame Corey for being excited. Mighty Mike was a popular disc jockey, known for his wicked sense of humor. Lots of kids listened to his program every Saturday, when he played the Top Ten songs and made jokes about them. Corey should have a wonderful time acting in the haunted house with Mighty Mike, and Corey's buddy, Nicholas, would surely be impressed.

"Corey says I'm going to get burned at the stake," she said.

"That's right," said Grandma. "You'll be Joan of Arc, Maid of Orleans."

"I've heard of her," Ellen said, "but I don't remember exactly what she did. Was she the one who heard voices and led the army into battle?"

Grandma nodded. "It should be one of our best scenes. You'll wear a long gown and be tied to the stake and the flames will leap around your bare feet."

"Oh, goodie," said Ellen.

"You won't really get burned, of course. They do everything with mirrors and tricks and optical illusions."

Corey hung up the phone. "The line's busy," he said.

"Who else is in my scene?" Ellen asked.

"I don't know. Mrs. Whittacker didn't say."

"That's all I do? Just stand there?"

"And scream," said Corey.

"There's a meeting of all the volunteers," Grandma said. "You'll be told then exactly what you're supposed to do."

"Maybe a movie producer will come," Corey said, "and he'll see me get my head chopped off and he'll hire me to scream in a horror movie." He raised his arms, with his hands like claws, made a horrible face, and lurched around the room.

"Mom and Dad won't let us go to horror movies," Ellen said, "so I doubt if they'd let you be *in* one."

Corey quit lurching. "They might, if I got paid thousands of dollars."

"The Historical Haunted House will be open from seven to ten for five days before Halloween," Grandma said, "so it will take quite a lot of your time. On Halloween night, it will be from six to midnight."

"I have to miss trick or treat," Corey said. "But it will be worth it."

Ellen agreed to help at the haunted house. It would be fun,

5

especially if she got to work with a celebrity like Mike McGarven. She could hardly wait to tell Caitlin. Ellen had never met anyone famous and she was quite sure none of her friends had, either.

Mrs. Streater came home then and heard all the details. While Grandma (and Corey) talked, Ellen wondered which celebrity would be in her scene.

"We get to scream," Corey said again. "Ellen screams while she burns and . . ."

"I don't think Joan of Arc screamed," Mrs. Streater said. "She prayed."

"Well, *I* get to scream while they chop off my head. The louder, the better."

"Just don't scream *after* you're supposedly beheaded," Grandma said. "Once the blade drops, you must lie completely still and be quiet."

"That'll be a first," said Ellen.

"It should be quite an event," Mrs. Streater said. "With so many radio and television personalities participating, the haunted house is certain to get lots of publicity."

"Mrs. Whittacker thinks the Historical Society will raise all the money they need to rewire the mansion," Grandma said. "We also hope that when people realize how many unusual items are in Clayton House—the furniture and the Wedgwood collection and all the rest—they will want to come back when the museum opens to see everything when it's properly lighted and displayed."

"What if the magic trick doesn't work right," Corey said, "and Ellen really catches on fire? The people watching would think Ellen's screams were part of the act. What if nobody untied her and . . ."

"Stop it," Ellen said, "or you'll *really* get your head chopped off."

"Nothing will go wrong with the magic tricks," Mrs. Streater said. "A real fire would be too dangerous; it will be a fake fire."

Ellen went to the kitchen to get a snack. As she took the first bite, Corey screamed—a shrill, bloodcurdling shriek that lasted several seconds.

Ellen jumped and dropped her banana. Prince, the Streaters' dog, whined and ran into the living room, sniffing the floor.

Ellen heard Grandma say, "Land's sakes, Corey! You scared me half out of my skin."

"Just practicing," Corey said.

"This family," said Mrs. Streater, "will be the death of me."

"Next time," said Grandma, "warn me before you practice."

Better yet, thought Ellen, don't practice at all.

"The orientation meeting is next Saturday morning," Grandma said, as Ellen returned. "I'll pick you up at nine o'clock. Mrs. Whittacker said if I bring you to the meeting, we can come early and she'll give us a personal tour of the mansion before the others arrive."

Ellen was glad to hear that Grandma would be there, too. Corey didn't mean to act up in public but he was so unpredictable. She never knew what he would say or to whom. If Ellen was going to be introduced to a lot of TV stars, she didn't want her little brother embarrassing her by making up one of his stories —or by deciding to practice his screaming in the middle of the meeting.

Chapter
2

Ellen peered through the windshield, eager for her first glimpse of Clayton House.

"I've driven past the Clayton property dozens of times," Grandma said. "I never thought I'd be on this side of the iron gates."

The long, curving driveway wound past a fountain. Water sprayed ten feet into the air while a sculpted cherub danced in the mist. Flower beds overflowed with gold and rust chrysanthemums; ducks and geese swam lazily on a pond.

"It's like a park," said Ellen.

"Forty acres," said Grandma.

"There's the house!" yelled Corey.

Grandma parked the car and they all gazed at the mansion.

As Ellen looked at turrets, gables, and several different kinds of chimneys, she felt a quick pang of apprehension. Clayton House seemed grim and unapproachable.

"It will be a perfect haunted house," said Grandma.

A porch with fancy pillars wrapped itself around the front of the house and a matching porch hugged the left side of the second story. A small balcony with an ornate wrought-iron railing extended from an upper room on the right side.

Grandma said, "Either the architect had a restless imagination, or else the house was designed by committee. The back doesn't seem to match the front and the sides are completely different from each other."

"I wish we lived here," said Corey. He pointed to the room with the balcony. "I'd take that room so I could sleep outside all summer."

Despite the parklike grounds, Ellen was glad she didn't live in Clayton House. But Grandma was right—it would be a great haunted house.

Mrs. Whittacker met them at the door. She led them into the great entry hall, where a huge staircase curved upward, its banisters intricately carved to resemble swans and cherubs. Sunlight streamed through a large stained-glass window, painting colored designs on the polished wooden floor. The walls were of wood, too, and all were carved in various designs.

"Samuel Clayton made his fortune in lumber," Mrs. Whittacker said. "When the mansion was built, his lumberyards were right next door." She waved her hand at the decorative woodwork. "He was one of the first to use steam-powered woodworking machinery. Previously, this sort of thing had to be done by hand. The machines made it so easy that Mr. Clayton got a bit carried away. He used fine wood throughout the house. Rosewood. Mahogany. Even satinwood."

"I never heard of satinwood," Ellen said.

"It's an East Indian tree." Mrs. Whittacker pointed to a yellowish-brown panel. "This is made of satinwood. Feel it."

Ellen touched it. The wood felt smooth and rich.

"Where do the wedge trees grow?" asked Corey.

"I beg your pardon?"

"The wedge trees. That the Wedgwood comes from."

Mrs. Whittacker managed not to laugh as she explained that Wedgwood is a fine earthenware, made by the Wedgwood Company in England.

"You mean *dishes*?" Corey said.

"That's right. You'll see the Wedgwood when we go upstairs, including some pieces which were made in the eighteenth century."

"Some are two hundred years old," said Grandma.

"Even older than you," said Corey.

"The Wedgwood collection is worth more than $200,000," said Mrs. Whittacker.

Ellen imagined living in such a building. The entryway alone was larger than the Streaters' entire house. It may be elegant, she thought, but it certainly isn't very homey.

All her life, Ellen had experienced strong feelings for places. When she went into a house, she knew if the people who lived there loved each other or if they were angry or afraid or sick. It wasn't something she could explain—in fact, she had never tried—but her feelings were invariably correct.

She had always disliked visiting a particular aunt and uncle because whenever she was in their home, it seemed filled with anger and the feeling made her uncomfortable. When the aunt and uncle divorced last year, her parents and grandparents were shocked. Ellen wasn't surprised; she sensed years ago that Uncle Ted and Aunt Cheryl did not like each other.

When she was only six, Ellen told her mother that a neighbor, Mrs. Lantow, was sick. When Mrs. Streater inquired, Mrs.

Lantow cheerfully said her health was fine. Months later, the Streaters learned that Mrs. Lantow had undergone chemotherapy treatments for cancer but had told no one.

Clayton House didn't contain feelings of anger or illness but Ellen sensed no love or joy, either. Despite the comfortable temperature, the house felt cold; with all the elegant furnishings, the mansion seemed empty. Something sinister hung in the air, as if the walls knew a secret evil that was not apparent to visitors.

Corey and Grandma were awed by the splendor; Ellen felt vaguely uneasy. She pushed the feeling aside and concentrated on Mrs. Whittacker's voice.

"The house was built in 1864," Mrs. Whittacker said. "At that time, Mr. Clayton used the lower level for his business. He had an office, meeting rooms, and a display room. The servants' quarters were also on this floor, along with a small kitchen and dining room. The main kitchen and dining room are upstairs, where the Clayton family lived."

Ellen had never heard of a house with more than one kitchen.

"There are four fireplaces on the lower floor," Mrs. Whittacker continued, "each one different." She guided them from room to room.

One fireplace was made of black and gray marble, imported from Italy. Another was a pale blue onyx, so translucent it seemed to be formed of wax. A third was surrounded by satinwood, heavily carved. Ellen's favorite was the one made from Mexican silver, with a hearth of white mahogany.

When Mrs. Whittacker led the way to the next room, Ellen lingered behind, admiring the silver fireplace. She wondered if the Claytons ever actually lit fires in their exquisite fireplaces. Flames would look lovely, reflected in the gleaming silver.

11

Lightly, she ran her fingers over the shiny metal, marveling at its beauty.

"Don't touch that!"

Ellen jerked her hand away and turned toward the harsh voice.

A middle-aged woman stood behind her.

"Silver tarnishes," the woman said.

"I'm sorry. I didn't mean to tarnish the silver. It's just so beautiful and I . . ."

"Well, keep your hands to yourself from now on," the woman snapped.

Ellen swallowed and twisted her fingers together, not sure if she should answer or not. She stared at the woman's excessive green eye shadow.

Grandma, Mrs. Whittacker, and Corey returned. "Oh, it's you, Agnes," Mrs. Whittacker said. "We heard voices; I thought perhaps Ellen had bumped into Lydia." She laughed, as if she had just told a joke.

The woman smiled graciously. "Your friend and I were having a cozy little chat."

Ellen quickly crossed the room and stood beside her grandmother. If that was a cozy little chat, she thought, I'd hate to have an argument with this woman.

Mrs. Whittacker said, "This is Agnes Munset, a talented artist who specializes in ceramics. She's agreed to be curator of the museum's Wedgwood collection."

"Don't you own the Potlatch Gallery?" Grandma asked, after the introductions were finished.

"Yes."

"I've been there many times," Grandma said. "I especially like your pansy vases. I've given several as wedding gifts."

The woman who had scolded Ellen was all sweetness and charm as she discussed her gallery and her art work. Ellen couldn't believe the transformation. Agnes even asked Corey how old he was and then told him he looked much older.

Corey beamed.

When Mrs. Whittacker led them upstairs, Ellen was glad Agnes Munset didn't follow.

As they neared the top of the stairs, Corey said, "Who's Lydia? You said you thought maybe Ellen had bumped into Lydia."

"I was just teasing Agnes," Mrs. Whittacker said. "Lydia is our ghost."

"Your *what?*" said Grandma.

"Oh, didn't I tell you? The mansion really *is* haunted."

"Now, Marie," said Grandma, "be serious."

Mrs. Whittacker winked at Ellen and Corey. "There *are* stories," she said, "that the ghost of Lydia Clayton, Samuel's first wife, was often seen around Clayton House in the years after her death."

"I hope I see her," Corey said.

"You might," Mrs. Whittacker said. "Lydia's ghost was here just last month."

"Have you seen her?" asked Grandma.

"No," Mrs. Whittacker admitted.

"I didn't think so. Has Agnes?"

"Agnes refuses to discuss the ghost. She says such supernatural prattling is beneath a woman of her talent and education. But the electrician who came to measure the dining room and give us an estimate for upgrading the wiring and installing spotlights swears he felt her presence." She paused and then added, "Of course, the electrician is also a member of our Historical

Society and he just happens to be in charge of publicity for the Historical Haunted House."

"And it would certainly be good publicity," Grandma said, "if rumors of a real ghost should start to circulate."

"Wouldn't it, though?" said Mrs. Whittacker.

"I hope I see Lydia," said Corey. "If I do, I'll ask her how it feels to be a ghost. Does it hurt when she goes through walls? Do ghosts ever eat? Are there animal ghosts, or only people? If I see her, I'm going to ask her if I can dress up like a ghost, in a sheet or something, and go with her to see where all the ghosts live. I bet she'd let me, if I promised to be really quiet for the whole day, so nobody noticed me."

There is no way, thought Ellen, that her brother could ever be really quiet for a whole day.

What did Mrs. Whittacker mean when she said the ghost was felt? Exactly how does one *feel* a ghost? Ellen frowned. She already sensed something menacing about the mansion. Her encounter with the museum's curator was upsetting, too, and now there was talk of a ghost. The huge old house, beautiful as it was, gave her the creeps.

"If you see the ghost," Corey said to Ellen, "send her to me. I'll ask her to visit my class at school."

"You are not going to see any ghost," Grandma said.

Ellen hoped she was right.

Chapter
3

Fairylustre. A perfect name, Ellen thought, as she gazed at the exquisite octagon-shaped bowl. The outside of the bowl showed a castle, with a bridge and archways in black, purple, green, and gold. The inside depicted winged fairies, outlined in gold. The fairies flew through the air, perched on toadstools, and hid from imps and other tiny people.

Ellen loved fairies. When she was little, her two favorite books had illustrations of fairies. She had asked to hear those stories so often that eventually she memorized them and "read" them to herself, long before she really knew how to read. She used to tape cloth wings to her dolls and pretend that they were the fairies in the stories, flying through the air. And three years in a row, she insisted on having a fairy costume for Halloween.

Ellen no longer played with dolls, but she kept a small glass fairy on her dresser, for good luck. She still had her fairy books, too. The octagonal bowl was even more beautiful than the illustrations in Ellen's books.

"You may hold it, if you like," Mrs. Whittacker said. "Until we have enough money to install spotlights, it's difficult to fully appreciate these pieces unless you pick them up."

Ellen hesitated. Mrs. Whittacker had said that even the small pieces of Fairylustre were appraised at more than two thousand dollars. What if she accidentally dropped it? Still, there was something compelling about the shimmering colors that made her want to touch them, and she longed to see the fairies up close. She picked up the bowl and turned it slowly around, examining each fairy. "It's beautiful," she whispered.

"The full name is Wedgwood Fairyland Lustre," Mrs. Whittacker said, "but it's usually shortened to Fairylustre. It was made between 1915 and 1931."

No wonder Mrs. Whittacker was excited about turning Clayton House into a museum. Treasures such as the silver fireplace, the carved banisters, and the Fairylustre should be displayed where people could enjoy looking at them.

Ellen laughed. "Look, Grandma," she said and she pointed to the shoes on a flying fairy.

Grandma looked and laughed, too. She told Mrs. Whittacker, "I've always said Ellen needs fairy shoes."

"I always wear out my tennis shoes on *top*," Ellen explained. "I get holes in them, right over my big toes. Mom accuses me of walking with my toes pointed straight up."

"Let me see the fairy shoes," Corey said.

"They point upward," Ellen said, as Corey bent over the bowl.

"Do you want to hold the bowl too, Corey?" Mrs. Whittacker asked.

Corey nodded. Ellen started to hand the bowl to him and

then stopped. The bowl was suddenly cold and a damp chill spread up her wrists.

Ellen stared at the bowl. It felt like a bowl sculpted of ice, with a fan behind it blowing the cold air toward Ellen.

"It's my turn," Corey said, reaching for the bowl.

Ellen handed it to him but the feeling of cold stayed on her arms. She watched her brother carefully. He didn't seem to notice anything unusual about the bowl. If he felt the cold, she was sure he would say something about it. Corey was not known for keeping still when anything unusual happened.

Corey held the bowl for only a moment. "You'd better take it back," he told Mrs. Whittacker. "Sometimes I get the dropsies."

As soon as the bowl was safely back on the shelf, the cold disappeared from Ellen's hands. She waited a moment and then touched the Fairylustre bowl. There was no cold air, no icy feeling. Ellen jammed her hands in her pockets and stepped away from the shelves of Wedgwood.

"Let's go see the pig," Corey said.

"What pig?" Ellen said.

"Some king of Norway was murdered in a pigpen," Corey said, "and that scene is going to have a real pig in it. Mom told me."

"I think Corey's more interested in the horror scenes than he is in fine old ceramics," Grandma said.

"The pig won't be here until the haunted house opens," Mrs. Whittacker said.

Ellen wondered if the pigpen murder was the scene that wasn't based on truth.

"The dining room is the only room of the mansion that won't be made into a scene from history," Mrs. Whittacker said.

17

"Instead, we'll display the Wedgwood collection and some of the finer pieces of furniture in here."

The rest of the volunteers began arriving then and everyone assembled in what Mrs. Whittacker called "the second drawing room" to get their instructions.

As soon as they were seated, Ellen nudged Corey with her elbow and whispered, "Did you feel anything odd when you held that bowl?"

"Like what?"

"It seemed cold to me. And while we were holding it, I felt a cold wind blowing on my arms."

"I didn't feel anything."

"Why did you give the bowl back so quickly?"

Corey shrugged. "I was afraid I'd drop it. And I wanted to see the pig."

Ellen didn't say anything else. She kept thinking of what Mrs. Whittacker had said about someone feeling the ghost's presence.

Corey apparently had the same thought because he suddenly shouted, "Maybe it was Lydia!" Everyone turned to look at him.

"Shhh!!" Ellen said.

"What?" said Grandma. "What was Lydia?"

"Oh, nothing," Ellen said. "Corey's just telling me one of his stories."

Grandma chuckled and the other people quit staring.

Corey whispered to Ellen, "Maybe the cold air you felt was really a ghost." Corey's eyes were wide and serious.

It made her nervous to have him say what she had been thinking. "It was probably just my imagination," she said. "Old houses like this give me the heebie-jeebies."

"Well, if you feel it again," Corey said, "tell me so I can feel it, too." He was thoughtful for a moment. "Don't tell Grandma," he said. "If Mom and Dad find out there's a real ghost here, they might not let us do the haunted house. Maybe we should keep the ghost a secret."

"We don't know that there is a real ghost," Ellen said. She did not point out that she wasn't the one who shouted Lydia's name to a roomful of people the second the idea popped into her mind.

"What are you two whispering about?" Grandma asked.

Corey and Ellen answered exactly together: "Nothing."

Ellen wished she hadn't told Corey about the cold feeling. He said he wanted to keep it a secret, but he always blurted out whatever came into his head. She wondered why she had felt the cold air and he didn't. Did she only imagine it? She would have to be careful or her parents would think she was making things up, the way Corey does.

While Mr. and Mrs. Streater encouraged Corey's imagination, they also worried that he would forget to distinguish between what was true and what wasn't. Mr. Streater often said he thought Corey had the potential to be a first-rate writer— and also the potential to be a first-rate liar.

Perhaps, Ellen decided, a door had opened, causing cold air to blow across her hands just when she held the Fairylustre bowl. Yes, that must be what had happened.

The meeting began. Mrs. Whittacker explained to the group of volunteers exactly how the Historical Haunted House would work. Ellen tried to listen carefully but it was hard to concentrate when there were so many well-known people in the room. She recognized two sportscasters, several TV news people, the weatherman from Channel Five, and a woman who did a cooking show that Ellen's mother sometimes watched.

A part of her mind kept thinking about the Fairylustre bowl and the cold wind.

Partway through the meeting, Ellen sensed that someone was watching her. When she glanced around, everyone in the room appeared to be looking straight at Mrs. Whittacker. Still, Ellen couldn't shake the feeling that someone was staring at her.

You're getting jumpy, she told herself, and the haunted house hasn't even started yet.

When the general instructions were finished, each person was told which room his or her scene would be in. Corey's scene was in the conservatory and Ellen's was in the parlor. Maps of the mansion were distributed. Ellen couldn't imagine living in a house so big that people needed maps to find their way around.

"Someone from the Historical Society will be in each room, to assist you," Mrs. Whittacker said. "Please find your assigned room and go there now."

"If you can find your own way," Grandma told Ellen, "I'll go with Corey to the conservatory."

Ellen studied the map. The parlor and the conservatory were both upstairs, across the hall from the main dining room where all the Wedgwood was displayed.

"We'll be in adjoining rooms," she told Corey.

"Good," he said. "You can meet Mighty Mike, too. I wonder what he looks like." Corey seemed to have forgotten all about the ghost of Lydia Clayton.

As Ellen walked toward the parlor, she wondered who else would be in her scene. One of the newscasters? The weatherman? The cooking school woman? Ellen entered the parlor and stopped in dismay as she saw which Historical Society member had been assigned to the Joan of Arc scene. Agnes Munset.

"Yours is the only scene with just one person," said Agnes.

"We all felt that extra actors would dilute the impact of watching young Joan burn at the stake."

Ellen tried to hide her disappointment. She wasn't going to work with a celebrity, after all.

"I'll tie you to the stake each night," said Agnes, "and I'll start the machine that makes the fake fire. Then I'll need to take care of other duties. I assume you know what you're supposed to do."

Ellen said, "I'm supposed to stand still and look saintly."

Agnes nodded. "That's exactly right," she said. "Let's try it once, to be sure everything works properly."

Scenery flats, painted to look like shop fronts and crowds of people, loomed across the back and both sides of the room, making it look like the village square of Rouen, France, in the year 1430. In the center of the scene, a pile of sticks and branches waited. If it had not been for the small platform in the middle of the pile—and the rough hewn 2 × 4 going straight up from the middle of the platform—the scene would have seemed like preparations for a homecoming bonfire or some other town celebration.

On the back of the platform, not seen from the public viewing area, three steps led upward. Ellen climbed them and stood on the platform with her back to the stake. It rose several feet above her head.

"Cross your arms and put your hands on your shoulders," Agnes said.

Ellen did.

Agnes tied Ellen to the 2 × 4 with rope. She wound the rope around Ellen, just below her shoulders, and again at the waist. Using another length of rope, she bound Ellen's ankles to the stake.

"It should be loose enough that you can wiggle out if you need to," Agnes said. "Of course, you shouldn't do that when there's an audience."

Even with the rope fairly loose, it made her feel helpless to be lashed to the stake.

Agnes flipped a switch and Ellen heard a crowd shouting. The angry voices filled the room.

"Witch!"

"Heretic!"

"Death to the traitor!"

Ellen's skin prickled.

When Mr. Streater had learned that Ellen and Corey were to be in the haunted house, he urged them to study the characters they played. Corey had not yet bothered to learn about Prince Rufus but Ellen had read everything she could find about Joan of Arc.

She learned that Joan was a French patriot and mystic who lived more than five hundred years ago. When Joan was in her teens, she believed she heard the voices of saints directing her to lead the French army against their English invaders. Obeying the voices, she inspired the soldiers and led the French to victory.

Then, during an attempt to liberate Paris, Joan was taken prisoner and accused of witchcraft. A church court condemned her. Before her death, she publicly declared the justice of France's cause and the authenticity of the voices she heard. Twenty-five years later, legal proceedings cleared her name and her condemnation was annulled. And in 1920, the Roman Catholic Church declared her a saint.

Ellen felt sorry for Joan of Arc. A lot of good it did to clear her name after they had already killed her.

Her only "crimes" were patriotism and a belief that she heard the voices of saints. Why were her accusers so angry?

When Ellen had asked her father about it, he said people can always find good reasons to do terrible deeds and that the real lesson of history is to stay calm and not be too quick to judge other people.

As she listened to the angry voices, Ellen wished the people who condemned Joan of Arc had not been so quick to judge.

Agnes hit another switch. As the lights dimmed, Ellen felt as if she stood in the middle of a fire. Red and yellow lights whirled at her feet in a way that made the pile of sticks appear to be burning. She heard the crackling of the flames, with the shouting crowd still in the background. To her amazement, she also smelled smoke.

"I can smell it!" she said.

"Several of the exhibits have smells as well as sight and sound," Agnes said. "Technicians from the Provincial Museum in Vancouver, British Columbia, helped us prepare them."

Ellen leaned her head against the stake and looked upward. Joan of Arc must have been terrified, with the flames leaping around her ankles and the wild crowd cheering as her clothing caught fire. How did she keep from struggling and screaming? How did she manage to stand there calmly and pray?

"It's perfect," Agnes said. She stood now in the viewing area, behind the ropes that would keep the public at the far end of the parlor. "You look exactly like Joan should look."

"Thanks." Perhaps, Ellen decided, she had judged Agnes too hastily. Maybe she wasn't mean, after all.

Agnes turned off all the special effects and untied the ropes. Since Ellen didn't have to practice with anyone else or rehearse any lines, she finished before Corey did.

While she waited for Grandma and Corey, Ellen went back into the dining room to look at the Fairylustre again. Each piece was different; each had exquisite colors. Not all of the Fairylustre pieces had fairy scenes, however. One had tiny drops of gold forming a spider web pattern. Another, a large vase, pictured a twisted, dry tree with demon's heads instead of leaves, and bats hanging on the branches. At the foot of the tree, a white rabbit with pink eyes, wearing a pink jacket, seemed to be running for his life. Ellen wondered if there were stories depicted on the Fairylustre or just random scenes.

Behind her, Ellen heard Corey's excited voice. "Wait till you hear me scream, Mighty Mike. I'm going to practice until I'm the best screamer in the world."

I hope he practices when I'm not around, Ellen thought.

She leaned close to the vase, noticing new details. As she did, she had the same sensation she'd had earlier, that someone was watching her. As she looked around at the empty room, she felt a sudden chilling breeze, as if someone had just opened a door or window directly beside her. A prickle of fear ran across her scalp.

Ellen straightened and backed away from the Wedgwood. There were no windows in this room and the only door was the one to the hallway. The cold air continued to brush against her. She shivered and turned to leave. The cold air swirled around her, surrounding her. Ellen stopped.

Was it a magic trick, something rigged up especially for the haunted house?

She took a deep breath, trying to control her pounding heart. Be logical, she told herself. She looked carefully around the dining room for any wires which might lead to concealed fans or air-conditioning vents. Maybe the electrician had fixed it so the air-conditioning system would produce sporadic blasts of frigid air. Maybe it was a publicity stunt. Mrs. Whittacker said the electrician was in charge of publicity.

But this room wasn't going to have a haunted house scene; this room was only a display of furniture and the Clayton family's Wedgwood collection. There would be no reason to scare people who came to admire the museum pieces.

The walls in the dining room were plainer than the rest of the mansion so that full attention could be focused on the rows of recessed china cupboards which held the Wedgwood collection. She saw no wires. No vents. No way to make a blast of cold air turn on and off.

It's the ghost, Ellen thought. It's the ghost of Lydia Clayton. The cold wind seemed to blow from all directions at once. Ellen wanted to run away from it but she felt as if roots had grown down through the bottoms of her feet and anchored her to the floor.

Maybe the electrician had not tried to start a rumor. Maybe when the electrician got close to the Wedgwood he was warned away by Lydia's ghost. Afterward, he was probably embarrassed when other members of the society laughed at his report of a ghost and so he pretended that he had made it all up as a way to get publicity.

"There you are!" Corey's voice at the dining-room door jarred Ellen into motion. The cold wind vanished. "Come and meet Mighty Mike," Corey called.

Ellen ran out of the dining room. Although the cold air did not follow her, she felt chillled to the bone, anyway.

"That's what I like," Mighty Mike said, as Ellen dashed toward him, "a fan who's eager to shake my hand."

When Ellen and Corey got home, they sat around the table

with their parents, eating tuna sandwiches, while Corey told all about the mansion and the pig and Mighty Mike. All, that is, except the part about a ghost. To Ellen's relief, Corey was too excited about Mighty Mike and about pretending to get his head chopped off to talk of anything else.

"You're awfully quiet," Mrs. Streater said to Ellen.

"She hasn't had a chance," Mr. Streater said, looking at Corey.

"Ellen felt the ghost!" Corey said.

Ellen kicked him under the table. She might have known he couldn't keep anything secret.

"I mean, there was a statue there and we pretended it was a ghost and Ellen . . ."

"Let Ellen tell her part herself," Mrs. Streater suggested.

"I'm alone in my scene," Ellen said, "but there are lots of special effects. You can even smell the fire."

"And there's weird music," said Corey. "It gets loud right when the big knife comes toward my head."

Ellen didn't mind letting Corey do the talking. She was anxious to be alone, to ponder what had happened. She needed to think about the cold wind that she thought was the ghost of Lydia Clayton.

After lunch, Ellen took a hot shower. The water poured over her, warming her at last.

The ghost was watching me, Ellen decided. I sensed it during the meeting and again in the dining room. She watched me and then she tried to—to what? To scare me away?

Why me? Ellen wondered. Out of all the dozens of celebrities and volunteers and Historical Society members who were at Clayton House today, why was I the only one who felt the ghost?

Chapter
4

As Mrs. Streater had predicted, the Historical Haunted House got plenty of publicity. Hundreds of tickets were presold. Many of Ellen's friends planned to attend and they all promised to come to the Joan of Arc scene. Caitlin said she would try to come more than once.

On opening night, the volunteers arrived two hours early, to allow time for a final dress rehearsal. The Historical Society had clearly been busy since the orientation meeting. The outside of the mansion was now shrouded in huge spider webs, making the building look as if the doors had been shut for a hundred years. Eerie music drifted across the grounds. The water in the courtyard fountain was green and slimy and the cherub in the center of the fountain was gone, replaced by an evil-looking sea serpent.

"I may not have to pretend I'm scared," Corey said, as they climbed the steps and entered the mansion. The entry hall was transformed. The carved woodwork and somber furniture which had seemed so impressive in the sunlight looked melancholy in the gloomy semidarkness. Strange sounds came from every direction: creaking doors, a muffled scream, the whoosh of unseen wings. Small eyes—rats? snakes?—glowed from corners and discordant music drifted down the great carved staircase.

Corey slipped his hand into Ellen's. She squeezed it, to reassure him, but she wished she could turn around and leave. Let somebody else stand in this creepy place every night for a week, tied to a stake.

Just then, the lights went on and Mrs. Whittacker's voice came over the loudspeaker. "By now, I'm sure you all can see how effective the Historical Haunted House is going to be. The lights will remain on for thirty minutes. All volunteers please take your places."

Ellen hurried to the parlor, put on her costume, and climbed to the platform where Joan of Arc would burn at the stake.

Her rehearsal went smoothly. First a woman from the Historical Society gave her some stage makeup and showed her how to apply it. There was foundation, eye shadow, blush, and lipstick.

"Without makeup," the woman explained, "you would look far too pale under the special lights. You're supposed to be Joan of Arc, not her ghost."

The casual remark annoyed Ellen. She did not want to think about ghosts.

"You may keep the makeup," the woman went on. "It will be more convenient for you to put it on at home each day before you come."

When the makeup woman left, Agnes tied the ropes around Ellen's ankles, waist and shoulders, turned on the various switches, and watched for a few minutes from the viewing area. Then she turned everything off, untied Ellen, and told her she was free to do whatever she wanted until she heard the announcement that it was time for all actors to take their places.

Ellen peeked into Corey's room. Mighty Mike, wearing a long black robe and a black hood, stood beside the guillotine. Corey lay with his head on a wooden block, grinning gleefully.

"Should I scream now?" Corey asked.

"Let's save the screaming for when we have an audience," Mighty Mike replied. "We wouldn't want you to overdo it and lose your voice."

Maybe *you* wouldn't, Ellen thought, but it would be a whole lot more peaceful at home.

While she waited, Ellen decided to see how she looked with the makeup on. She remembered seeing an ornately framed mirror in the room where the Wedgwood was. She entered the dining room and looked in the large oval mirror which hung just inside the door. She had never worn makeup before and she thought the eye shadow made her eyes seem enormous. She wondered how Corey felt about wearing makeup.

She left the mirror and wandered over to the Wedgwood display. Some of the older pieces, such as the black basalt, got only quick glances. Mrs. Whittacker said it was old, expensive and highly collectible, but Ellen didn't think it was particularly pretty. Other pieces, like the creamware, were much more attractive but she didn't look at them long, either. She focused her attention on the Fairylustre. She was drawn to it, feeling connected on a deep level, as if she herself had painted the small green fairies and embellished their long, sweeping wings with gold.

She stood warily for a moment, wondering if the chill breeze would appear. It did not. Ellen relaxed and began to admire the fairies.

The Wedgwood was carefully arranged by date, with a small brass plaque identifying each piece. The earliest was a large black urn. The plaque said it was made in 1768. Next was a set of cream-colored dishes with a rose and green design on the border. The Fairylustre was much newer. Ellen wasn't interested in any of the other patterns or types of Wedgwood, only the Fairy-lustre. Of course, the dim lighting, which had been designed for formal candlelight dinners in the old dining room, did not show the pieces to the best advantage. It was easy to see why Mrs. Whittacker planned to use some of the haunted house profits to install spotlights.

Ellen's favorite piece, the small octagonal bowl, was tipped slightly, so that viewers could see the inside as well as the outside. Ellen longed to hold it again but she didn't dare pick it up without permission.

For the first time, she realized why people have collections. She began to understand why someone would care so much about an old bowl that they would pay thousands of dollars for it. If I were rich, she thought, I would buy a piece of Fairylustre with fairies on it. She liked the vase where a spider web was made entirely of tiny gold dots, too, but the pieces that showed the fairies were the ones she liked most.

The purple, green, and gold colors of the fairyland scene on the octagonal bowl were truly lustrous. Even in the dim light, they shimmered and Ellen thought she had never seen anything so beautiful. She wished she could meet the artist; clearly it was someone who loved fairies as much as Ellen did.

The voice of Agnes Munset came over the loudspeaker. "Ten minutes until we open. All actors please take your places. Ten minutes until we open."

Ellen took one last look at the octagonal Fairylustre bowl, trying to imprint every detail on her memory so that she could think about it later.

Then she turned and hurried toward the door. As she did, she caught a glimpse of movement in the mirror. When she looked, two faces gazed back at her from the mirror, her own and another.

Ellen glanced back over her shoulder, wondering who was behind her. The room was empty.

With her heart racing, she looked at the mirror again. The other face was still there. It was a young woman with light brown curls, wearing a long-sleeved, white nightgown with lace at the throat. She might have been pretty except for the expression on her face. Ellen had never seen anyone look so sad.

Her unhappy eyes stared straight at Ellen and her mouth slowly opened, as if she wanted to cry out for help but could not speak. Her arms lifted and her hands stretched toward Ellen, beseeching her to—to what? To help her? How?

Ellen stood still, unable to move or speak. The back of her neck prickled as she stared at the face in the mirror.

Agnes's voice came again. "All actors should now be in their places."

Ellen glanced quickly around the room again. She was still alone. When she looked back at the mirror, she saw only her own reflection. The sad woman had disappeared.

Ellen hurried across the hall. As she took her place on the platform in the Joan of Arc scene, her breath came fast, as if she'd been riding her bike uphill. The face in the mirror had to be one of the special effect tricks that had been set up throughout the haunted house. Still, it had startled her so much that her heart was still pounding. She wondered how they could make the face so realistic. For a moment, Ellen had been convinced that the woman was standing directly behind her.

Before they left for home that night, Ellen took Corey into the dining room to show him the face in the mirror. She didn't tell him about it; she wanted it to surprise him, the way it had surprised her.

She led him in, pretending she wanted to show him a fairy scene on one of the dishes. "See the mushrooms?" she said. "And the toadstools? I think the fairies use them for chairs."

Corey glanced at the Fairylustre without really looking. "Mighty Mike is going to the Rose Bowl game this year," he said, "and he's going to ride a horse in the parade. He gets to go the week before and see how they make the floats for the parade. He says they make whole scenes out of flowers. I have to watch the Rose Bowl parade on television because I might see him and if the camera is pointed at him, he'll wave to me."

Ellen turned away from the Fairylustre and started toward the door. There she was again. The sad woman in the mirror was behind her, arms outstretched, beseeching. Ellen waited for Corey to notice but he just kept chattering about Mighty Mike's visit to the Rose Bowl parade.

Ellen stopped walking and pointed at the mirror. "Look," she said.

Corey looked up. "What?" he said.

"See the woman? I wonder how they do that."

"What woman?"

"The woman in the mirror."

"I don't see any woman in the mirror."

Ellen looked at Corey to see if he might be teasing her. Then she looked at the mirror again. She saw her own face. To the left, and not quite as tall, was Corey's face. And in between them, taller than both, was the woman in the nightgown.

"You don't see her, standing between us?" Ellen said.

Corey shook his head. "All I see is you and me. Is it supposed to be a trick mirror?"

"Change places with me," Ellen said. "Stand where I'm standing and then look."

They traded places. Ellen could still see three faces in the mirror. "Do you see her now?" she asked.

"Nope. They've probably turned it off for tonight."

Ellen stared at her brother. Why couldn't Corey see the face? Ellen saw the curls and the nightgown and the sad eyes just as clearly as if the woman had been standing directly beside her. She saw the hands, stretching toward Ellen, as if begging her to grab hold.

"Let's go," Corey said. "Mom will be waiting for us and I'm hungry and I want to tell her about the Rose Bowl parade."

Silently, Ellen followed her brother out of the room. It was not, she knew, a trick mirror. A trick mirror would work for everyone, not just for one person.

Mrs. Whittacker stood by the front door when Ellen and Corey went down the stairs. "You're the last to leave tonight," she told them.

"We were in the dining room," Corey said. "Ellen wanted to show me the trick mirror but it was already shut off."

"What trick mirror?" said Mrs. Whittacker. "There isn't any trick mirror in the dining room. We didn't put any haunted house scenes in the dining room because we don't want to distract attention away from the displays."

"I was only kidding," Ellen said.

Mrs. Whittacker went out with them and, using a key,

locked the door. "We had a special deadbolt installed," she said, "so it takes a key to unlock the door, even from the inside. With so many people coming through the mansion, we thought it best to take some security precautions."

"Aren't you going to turn off the lights?" asked Corey. "It would waste energy to leave them on all night."

"They're on a timer. They all go out automatically in half an hour."

"There's Mom," Ellen said.

Corey dashed to the car and began telling his mother about Mighty Mike's trip to the Rose Bowl.

Ellen rode home in silence. Twice, she had seen a woman in the mirror. Who? Lydia Clayton? That was the most sensible explanation, if you could call it sensible to see a ghost. Was it possible for a ghost's image to show up in a mirror even when the ghost itself was invisible? Why couldn't Corey see it? Why didn't the bowl feel cold to him when he touched it?

Until she got involved in the haunted house, Ellen had never thought much about ghosts. She wasn't sure if she believed in them or not. She didn't know anything about them, really.

But she knew one thing: the face she saw in the mirror was not her imagination. It was real.

Chapter
5

Ellen had a plan.

The second night of the haunted house, she headed straight for the dining room. If she saw the woman in the mirror again, she would ask Mrs. Whittacker to look at the mirror. Surely Mrs. Whittacker would see the woman's reflection, too.

If Mrs. Whittacker didn't see it, Ellen wasn't sure what she would do. She didn't have to decide, because when she looked in the mirror, she saw only herself. She waited a moment but nothing happened. She walked away and came back to the mirror. She still saw only her own reflection. She didn't have to show Mrs. Whittacker, after all. With relief, she turned her attention to the Fairylustre.

Again, she was drawn to the octagonal bowl with the paintings of the fairies. She remembered how, as a little girl, she had read her fairy books over and over, unable to get enough of them. She felt the same way now; she wanted to hold the bowl and to examine the fairies up close.

As she looked at the bowl, the room seemed suddenly cold and damp. Ellen shivered and hugged herself for warmth. The cold air intensified but it was all on her face, not her back, and she realized it came from the shelves of Wedgwood.

She squinted at the shelves, trying to figure out exactly where the icy blast originated.

Then she gasped. Her hands flew to her mouth and she stepped backward.

Two transparent hands floated up from inside the large black urn that was the oldest piece of Wedgwood in the Clayton collection. They were a woman's hands with tapered fingernails and they looked absolutely real, except that Ellen could see right through them.

Slowly the hands drifted toward Ellen. The fingers were outstretched, the way the hands of the woman in the mirror had been, as if the owner of the hands was begging.

Ellen took another step backward. The hands followed. They floated toward Ellen, the fingers rippling slowly, as if they were somehow pulling themselves through the air.

With a shock, Ellen realized that the hands were the source of the icy air. The chill wind blew out of them, straight toward her. Instead of blowing past her, as an ordinary breeze would, it doubled back, swirling around her face and shoulders, lifting her hair and then letting it fall again.

Ellen tried to speak, to tell the hands to go away, but her mouth felt glued shut. She wanted to scream for help but she couldn't. She was unable to utter a sound. She felt like a statue, fastened in concrete to that spot in the floor, unable to move or speak.

The hands came closer. The air grew colder.

One of the hands reached toward Ellen's face, as if to touch her. When the fingers were almost to her cheek, Mrs. Whittacker's voice announced, "Ten minutes until we open. All actors in place, please."

The sound jarred Ellen free from her fear. With a great burst of energy, she turned and ran out of the room. As she passed the mirror, she saw a reflection of the hands. They were floating back toward the shelves. Ellen looked behind her. The hands disappeared inside the black urn.

It was the ghost. Ellen had no doubt about that. Even the clever people who had designed the haunted house could not invent floating hands with cold air blowing out of them.

Agnes was waiting to start the Joan of Arc sound effects when Ellen rushed into the room.

Ellen stopped, her heart beating a rapid rhythm as she caught her breath.

"What's wrong?" Agnes asked. "You're white as a ghost."

"The ghost isn't white; she's transparent," Ellen said. "I saw her—the real ghost—over there, in the dining room. I was looking at the Fairylustre and two hands came floating up out of a big urn. I felt cold air and I could see right through the hands. She tried to touch me. The hands reached for my face." The memory of it made Ellen shudder.

Agnes stared at Ellen for a long moment. "Let me be sure I understand," she said. "You believe you saw a pair of hands come out of the Wedgwood?"

"Yes! I swear it really happened."

"Where are the hands now?"

"When I ran away, the hands went back inside the urn."

"I see."

Ellen could tell that Agnes was skeptical. "I saw the ghost last night, too," Ellen said. "Only last night it was a whole person, not just hands, and I saw her in the mirror by the dining-room door."

"You saw a woman's reflection?"

"Yes, but when I turned around, no one was there."

Agnes was silent for a moment, as if trying to decide what she should say. Finally she said, "Why do you keep going back to the dining room, if it scares you?"

"I like to look at the fairy scenes. The dining room doesn't scare me; it's the ghost that scared me. Why don't you believe me?"

"I just spent five minutes listening to your brother insist that purple people from Jupiter will land on the balcony outside the parlor tonight. Now you tell tales of ghost hands in the Wedgwood."

"Corey's always making up stories. This really happened."

"I told Mrs. Whittacker it was a mistake to have children in the haunted house, but she was determined to use the two of you. I can still find someone else to be Joan of Arc, if you're upset. Should I?"

Ellen hesitated. She knew Agnes hoped she would say yes, and she was tempted. It would be comforting to go home tonight and not come back—but she had told all of her friends to come and see her be Joan of Arc. She couldn't tell Caitlin that she was dropping out and she couldn't let Mrs. Whittacker down; Mrs. Whittacker was counting on her. Besides, she could just hear Corey if she quit doing the Historical Haunted House because she was afraid of a ghost. Everyone in three counties would hear all about it and, since nobody else had seen the ghost, they would think Ellen was just jittery.

"No," she said slowly. "I don't want to quit; I want to be Joan."

"Well, stay away from the dining room, since you don't seem to have a problem anywhere else. Now let's get your hands tied so I can turn things on in here. It's almost seven o'clock and people are lined up waiting to get in."

Ellen stood with her back against the stake and crossed her arms against her chest. She felt the rope as Agnes loosely tied it around her shoulders.

"Staying out of the dining room won't make the ghost go away," Ellen said.

"Nearly three hundred people went through the haunted house last night," Agnes said. "Most of them stopped in the dining room and not a single person said anything about any ghost."

"Then why have I seen it twice?"

"*If* you've seen it twice, both times in the dining room, I should think you would stay out of there. You know what the Wedgwood collection looks like; don't look at it anymore."

It seemed an odd remark from the woman who was curator of the new museum. Shouldn't she encourage people to look at the Wedgwood—to study it and appreciate it?

"If you have any more problems," Agnes continued, "I'll speak to your parents about finding a replacement."

Agnes flipped the switches which started the Joan of Arc scene. The flames seemed to leap and dance around Ellen's feet. The noise of fire crackling and voices shouting filled the room. Usually, the realistic sound track for the Joan of Arc scene transported Ellen backward in time. This time, she hardly heard it.

When the first group of haunted house patrons entered, Ellen closed her eyes and tilted her head back, the way she always did, as if she were beseeching God to save her. But she wasn't thinking about Joan or about burning at the stake.

Behind her closed eyelids, she saw a pair of ghostly hands, moving slowly toward her face, trying to touch her.

Ellen pondered what to do. If she told her parents, she knew they would insist that both she and Corey drop out of the haunted house. If they believed she had seen the ghost, they would want to protect her from any further encounters. If they didn't believe her, they would want to protect her from her own imagination. Either way, Ellen would feel like a baby. And Corey would be outraged if he had to give up his chance to scream with Mighty Mike.

She knew her parents loved her and they always tried to do what was best for her. She also knew that sometimes she had to solve her own problems. She had been terrified when she saw the hands. If she ran away now, she would feel cowardly and defeated. She would always wonder if she gave in too easily.

But how does one stand up to a ghost? How could she conquer her fear?

Knowledge.

The word popped into her mind as if it had been caught behind a trapdoor and had just sprung loose. Knowledge. Grandma always said that people fear the unknown. They are afraid of different cultures, of new ideas, of religions that depart from the safety of what they have been taught.

I will learn about ghosts, Ellen decided. I will learn about Lydia Clayton. If I see those hands again, I'll be prepared. I'll pay close attention to exactly how they look and what they do. Maybe I should start a journal, the way I kept track of my experiments in animal communication. She could imagine what the Science Fair judges would think of an experiment in human/ghost communication.

At closing time, Ellen asked Mrs. Whittacker how she could learn more about the Clayton family.

"There are some old diaries," Mrs. Whittacker said.

"Could I read them?"

"Of course. But you'll have to do it at the Historical Society's library. We don't allow any one-of-a-kind volume to leave."

She gave Ellen the address and told her the library was open on Saturdays from noon until four.

Ellen looked to see if Corey was ready to leave. He was still helping Mighty Mike clean up their scene and prepare the fake blood for the next day.

She glanced across the hall toward the dining room. What would happen if she waited for Corey in there? Would the ghost appear? She inched toward the door. The dining room was empty.

Actors from other scenes chatted as they left for the night. Ellen heard Mighty Mike's booming laugh. There are people nearby, she thought. They would hear me if I had to yell for help.

She threw back her shoulders and walked toward the shelves of Wedgwood. She stopped in front of the Fairylustre display.

Almost immediately, she felt the icy air. It swirled toward her, surrounded her, and then seemed to condense, to draw into itself. Ellen felt as if she were being sucked into the center of a small hurricane.

The wind stopped as quickly as it had begun. At the same moment, Ellen felt an icy hand on her shoulder. The individual fingers gripped her through her blouse but when she looked, she saw nothing.

"What do you want?" Ellen whispered.

A second hand touched her other shoulder. Together they pushed Ellen forward until she stopped at the rope which kept the public away from the Wedgwood.

Ellen knew that the ghost of Lydia Clayton wanted her to look at the Wedgwood.

The cold pressure increased, pushing on Ellen's shoulders until she ducked under the rope and stood directly in front of one of the Fairylustre vases. She leaned down until her face was only a few inches from the shelf.

Despite her closeness to the beautiful vase, Ellen hardly saw the lustrous colors or the golden spider webs. She could think only of the cold fingers on her back.

"Get away from there!"

At the sound of Agnes's voice, the cold hands evaporated, leaving a tingly feeling on Ellen's shoulders.

Ellen clutched the rope, feeling unsteady, as she turned to face Agnes.

"You have no business being inside that rope," Agnes said. "That's how things get broken."

Ellen nodded and ducked under the rope, away from the Wedgwood.

"What are you doing in here?"

"Waiting for my brother."

"You can wait for him in the conservatory. I thought we agreed that you wouldn't come in the dining room anymore."

"I wasn't scared this time."

"Well, it's after ten; this room is closed. And even if it weren't, I don't ever want you to go behind the rope again. Is that clear?"

"Yes."

"I mean it, Ellen. If I find you in here again, you'll be

replaced as Joan of Arc. I will tell Mrs. Whittacker that you can't be trusted to stay away from the Wedgwood."

Ellen didn't know what to say so she was silent. She let go of the rope and walked toward the door. As she passed Agnes, the woman put out a hand to detain her. "Why were you leaning so close just now? Why were you examining that vase?"

Ellen was not about to tell her the real reason—that she was leaning toward the vase because she felt two icy invisible hands on her shoulders, pushing her that way. If she did, she knew there would be someone else playing Joan of Arc tomorrow.

Instead, she said, "No particular reason. That's just where I happened to be standing."

Agnes's frown softened slightly. A flicker of emotion flashed across her face. Relief? But why did she care which piece of Fairylustre Ellen admired? There was something odd about this conversation, something that didn't quite make sense. Maybe Agnes had seen the ghost, too, but didn't want to admit it. Maybe she was afraid that Ellen would tell and that it would somehow have a bad effect on the museum.

Ellen tried to think it through on the way home but it was hard to concentrate with Corey chattering from the back seat.

"Mighty Mike says he'll take me to the radio station someday when he isn't working and take me in the studio and show me where he plays the Top Ten songs every Saturday. And he says he'll show me where they broadcast the news. And he's even going to buy me lunch at the cafeteria, where all the radio and TV guys eat."

"He must have taken quite a shine to you," said Mrs. Streater.

"He says I scream better than anyone and that if they ever

43

do a mystery on the radio and they need someone to scream, he's going to call me."

Lulled by the rhythm of the windshield wipers, Ellen began to relax. She tuned out Corey's voice—something she had learned, from necessity, to do with ease—and replayed in her mind the scenes in the Clayton mansion.

Lydia Clayton's icy hands had pushed Ellen toward the Wedgwood collection because she wanted Ellen to look closely at it. Why?

There's something she wants me to see, Ellen decided. Some piece in particular? Maybe there is one piece that was her favorite and she wants to make sure I notice it.

Tomorrow, Ellen decided, I'll go to the Historical Society and ask to read those old diaries.

If she knew more about Lydia Clayton, she might be able to figure out what the ghost was trying to tell her.

Chapter
6

What secrets would the diaries divulge? What would she learn about Lydia Clayton? Ellen arrived at the Historical Society's office promptly at noon the next day, filled with anticipation. She asked to see the Clayton family diaries, hoping she might soon understand the strange events at Clayton House.

The woman in charge hesitated, as if debating whether to trust Ellen with the diaries.

"Mrs. Whittacker suggested that I read them," Ellen said, "and I'll be careful."

The woman nodded and brought the diaries to Ellen.

There were three slim volumes, each with a soft leather cover embossed in gold. The pages inside were a thin parchment, yellowed with age. The writing had been done with brown ink, in a flowery script. The first letter of each paragraph was double size and full of curlicues.

Ellen carried the diaries to a table and began to read. Some of the writing was difficult to read and the language was hard to understand. Ellen hadn't known the English language had changed so much. After an hour of straining her eyes and her brain, Ellen closed the first volume and paged through the others, feeling discouraged.

She had hoped that the diaries would be personal accounts of life at Clayton House, perhaps written by Lydia herself. Instead, most of the diary entries were about the interior of the house and the furniture. All were signed by someone named Franklin Haller. Since Mr. Haller included details of cost and shipping arrangements for the furniture, the diaries read more like a designer's ledger than a personal history. Ellen wished she had gone for a bike ride with Caitlin instead of coming here.

"Did you find what you were looking for?" asked the woman who worked in the library.

Ellen shook her head. "I wanted to read about Lydia Clayton," she said.

The woman's eyes twinkled. "Do you like ghost stories?" she said, and then laughed at Ellen's surprised look. "You aren't the first to be fascinated by the reports of Lydia's antics," she said. She walked to a shelf of books, reached up, and removed one. Handing it to Ellen, she said, "Try this. It's a short biography of Lydia Clayton and includes the stories about her ghost."

"Thank you."

As she read, Ellen was fascinated by the woman who had lived so long ago. Lydia was only sixteen in 1866 when she married Samuel Clayton and went to live in his grand mansion. A spoiled girl who was used to having her own way, she threw a fierce temper tantrum the first time her husband went to England on a business trip. To placate her, he brought her a gift —a set of creamy white dishes with a hand-painted green and rose border design. The dishes were creamware, made by Wedgwood, and Lydia fell completely in love with them.

After that, the only gift she ever wanted was more Wedgwood and she devoted much of her time to her collection. She studied the old pieces and cataloged her new ones. "Her Wedgwood," according to the biographer, "was her passion and her delight."

Lydia and Samuel Clayton had a son they named Josiah, after Josiah Wedgwood. Lydia adored her baby and spent every waking moment with him. When little Josiah died of whooping cough at the age of four months, Lydia was inconsolable and never fully recovered from her grief. She became a recluse, spending all of her time with her beloved Wedgwood.

A year after Josiah's death, another son, Paul, was born. It was a difficult birth which left Lydia weak and ill. When Paul was only six weeks old, Lydia got pneumonia and died. On her death bed, she made her husband promise that he would always keep her Wedgwood.

Ellen pitied Lydia Clayton. She lost her first baby and didn't live to raise her second one. The unfortunate girl lived in the mansion only five years, and died when she was just twenty-one.

Ellen continued to read. Two years after Lydia's death, Samuel Clayton remarried. The union turned out to be an unhappy one. His new wife, Caroline, desiring to decorate the mansion to her own tastes, sold the Wedgwood collection, without her husband's knowledge, to a wealthy land baron who intended to give it to his daughter as a dowry.

When the land baron's workman arrived to pack the Wedgwood, he was forced out of the room by what he described as "a cold hurricane of such force that I thought the roof would fly off the house."

Once outside, the weather was calm and sunny but the worker refused to go back inside and try again. Insisting that supernatural forces were at work in the Clayton mansion, he believed he had been given a clear mandate not to pack the Wedgwood.

The land baron cancelled the deal, and Samuel Clayton found out what had happened. He forbade Caroline to sell the Wedgwood and he continued to add to the collection until his own death.

The incident with the land baron's workman was the first of what would be many reports of cold winds, moans in the night, and fleeting apparitions in the Clayton mansion. Local people, many of them jealous of the Clayton family's wealth, gossiped that Lydia Clayton's ghost was still guarding her worldly treasures, even after death.

The reports of hauntings continued for several years, with Caroline the main victim. Caroline, already jealous of her pretty predecessor, complained bitterly to Samuel that Lydia's spirit refused to leave Clayton House. More than once, Caroline tried to pack the Wedgwood away in storage, hoping that Samuel wouldn't miss it. He always noticed and insisted it be returned to its original shelves.

Caroline never had children and when she suffered a miscarriage, she told Samuel that it was caused by a fall she took as she fled from Lydia's ghost. Since no one witnessed the fall, there was no proof of her story, but Samuel, who longed for another child, decided to have Lydia's coffin dug up and burned. He intended to put Lydia's cremated remains in the Wedgwood and told Caroline, "She loved those dishes more than she loved me. She wants them in death, just as she always wanted them in life."

Caroline, however, refused to have Lydia's remains in the house and so Samuel gave up the plan.

Reports of ghost sightings continued to plague Samuel until his death from smallpox in 1895. He often blamed Caroline for the hauntings, saying that if she had allowed Lydia to be cremated and her remains placed in the Wedgwood, the ghost would quit haunting Clayton House. Caroline also died of smallpox, just a week after Samuel.

Years later, Samuel's great-grandson developed a passion for Wedgwood. "In particular," the book said, "Edward Clayton was fond of a new Wedgwood line called Fairyland Lustre. More than once, he declared that his great-grandmother, Lydia, would have liked the brilliant colors and the imaginative scenes."

Ellen reread that paragraph three times. Even though the pieces in the collection were dated, it had not occurred to her until now that Lydia Clayton lived long before the Fairylustre was made. If Lydia had never owned any of it, why would her ghost care about it now? Why did the hands push Ellen toward it, as if she wanted to be sure Ellen noticed it?

Whatever his feelings about Lydia's ghost, Samuel Clayton kept his promise about the Wedgwood. In his Last Will and Testament, he made sure his heirs would honor Lydia's request, as well. He left the mansion to his son, Paul, on condition that the entire Wedgwood collection must stay right where it was.

Paul not only followed his father's command, he perpetuated it in *his* will, and his heirs did the same. Samuel's great-grandson, Edward, was the last of the Clayton line. The book didn't say so, but Ellen knew he was the one who left the mansion to the city, to be managed by the Historical Society. Ellen wondered if the gift had specified that the famous collection of Wedgwood be kept or whether the Historical Society had made that choice.

After Samuel and Caroline died, there were no further reports of a ghost. The gossips of the time decided that it wasn't the Wedgwood Lydia wanted, it was her husband. The writer of the book agreed, claiming that, with the death of her husband, Lydia's restless spirit was finally at peace and her ghost was gone forever.

Ellen turned to the copyright page of the book. It was published in 1945. What had happened in the decades since then?

Were there other, unreported ghost sightings? Too bad no members of the Clayton family were still alive. The people who had lived in Clayton House would be the logical ones to see a ghost, if she appeared. But if Lydia's ghost had been seen, surely there would be some mention of it in newspapers.

Fleeting apparitions, the book said. It was a perfect description of the reflection of the woman in the mirror.

Ellen asked the Historical Society woman if this book was the most recent publication there was about Lydia Clayton.

The woman nodded. "From time to time, rumors of a ghost circulated, but none were ever documented. Eventually, they always faded away."

What did the ghost want, Ellen wondered, more than a century after her death? Why, after so many years without any proof of a ghost, would Ellen feel the icy wind which had chilled the land baron's workman so long ago?

The Wedgwood, of course. The reason was somehow connected to Lydia's treasured collection. But surely she would not object to showing the Wedgwood in a museum setting. The pieces were in no danger; they were beautifully displayed. As soon as the Historical Society spent the haunted house money, the Wedgwood would have special lights, to show it off even more. If the ghost truly loved these dishes, she should be happy to see people admiring them.

Ellen thanked the woman for letting her read the books. As she rode the bus home, she decided to go to the mansion early that night, to give herself time to examine the Wedgwood exhibit before she dressed in her Joan of Arc costume. Corey wouldn't mind going early. If he could, he would take his sleeping bag and stay at the haunted house all night.

Until now, Ellen had been interested only in the Fairylustre. She was attracted to the fairies, not the dishes themselves. Now, after reading about Samuel and Caroline and the ghost, Ellen was interested in all the Wedgwood and eager to study the older pieces. She would have to be careful, though. She couldn't let Agnes catch her in the dining room again.

Chapter
7

Everything went wrong.

Corey agreed to go an hour early that night but when Ellen told her mother, Mrs. Streater said, "You'll have to check with Grandma and Grandpa. We have tickets for the Seattle Repertory Theatre tonight so Grandma and Grandpa will drive you to the haunted house and pick you up afterward. What time do you want to leave?"

"Five o'clock. That would get us there at five-thirty instead of six-thirty."

"All right," Mrs. Streater said. "Be sure Grandpa and Grandma don't have to wait around with you. They're planning to go out to dinner after they drop you off."

When Ellen tried to reach her grandparents, she got their telephone answering machine. She left a message but they didn't call back. She tried two more times, just in case they were home but had forgotten to check the machine; each time she got the recording.

At five-thirty, she gave up. Grandpa and Grandma were scheduled to pick them up at six and obviously they had gone somewhere else first. She would just have to find a different time to study the Wedgwood.

When they arrived at the haunted house, they were astonished to see a long line of people waiting to get in.

"Looks like you're going to be busy tonight," Grandpa said.

"Mighty Mike's been talking about it on the radio," Corey said.

"This is wonderful," Grandma said. "They'll easily raise enough money to finish renovating the mansion. And I'm so proud of you two for all the time you're putting in. Grandpa and I brag to all our friends about it."

Ellen raced to the parlor and hurried into her costume. She had already applied her makeup at home and had helped Corey with his, too. She was all ready fifteen minutes before the doors opened. Just time to sneak across to the dining room and take a good close look at the big urn that the hands came out of.

But when she stepped out the parlor door, she nearly bumped into Agnes.

"Where are you going?" Agnes asked.

"To check on Corey," Ellen said. "Mighty Mike wasn't here yet when we arrived so I thought I'd better make sure their scene is ready."

"Mike's here," Agnes replied. "It's a good thing, too. You should see the crowd outside. If we can get everyone in place, we're going to open the doors early. Come on, I'll get your scene started."

Reluctantly, Ellen climbed up the steps to the platform and waited for Agnes to tie her to the stake. Agnes worked quickly, pulling the rope tighter than usual. She flipped the switches, said, "See you later," and left.

So much for coming early to look at the Wedgwood, Ellen thought. Maybe she would be able to sneak over to the dining room for a few minutes afterward.

The haunted house ran overtime. It seemed like half of King County decided to come that Saturday night. Instead of closing the doors at ten, it was 10:20 when the last visitors finally shuffled out. The time passed quickly for Ellen as she listened to what people viewing the scene said about it. Parents sometimes explained to children who Joan of Arc was and many people shrieked in horror at the idea of someone being burned alive.

That night was especially fun because Caitlin and some of Ellen's other school friends came. Although Ellen could not distinguish faces in the dim light, she recognized their voices. It took willpower not to smile when she heard Caitlin squeal, "Look! Ellen's on fire! Oh, I can't watch!"

Usually, Ellen could slip out of the rope at closing time, whether it was tied or not. That night, the rope was too tight. She had to wait for Agnes to come and untie her. She tapped her foot impatiently. Why had Agnes been so careless when she tied the rope?

An uncomfortable thought struck Ellen. Had Agnes tied her this tight on purpose, so she couldn't leave the room without Agnes knowing it? Was this Agnes's way of guaranteeing that Ellen didn't go back in the dining room? Why would she care whether Ellen got scared or not? Certainly not because she was fond of Ellen.

54

Mrs. Whittacker made an announcement on the loud-speaker: "Everyone please leave as quickly as possible tonight."

I'd love to, Ellen thought. She heard other actors talking and hurrying past the door to the parlor. She didn't call to them to untie her because she expected Agnes to arrive any second. When Agnes didn't appear, Ellen wished she had asked someone else to help her but by then the hall outside the parlor was empty. Where was Corey? He could untie her. You would think her brother would come to look for her.

When Agnes finally came, she looked surprised to see Ellen.

"I thought you'd be on your way home by now," she said.

"I can't get loose. The rope is too tight."

"Oh, my," Agnes said. "I'm so sorry. I certainly did not intend to tie the rope that tight." She quickly untied Ellen and apologized again. Ellen felt guilty for suspecting that Agnes had done it on purpose.

Agnes walked out of the room with Ellen and accompanied her down the stairs to the great hall. Corey was waiting for her there.

"I wondered where you were," he said.

"I couldn't get untied."

"Oh. I thought you were probably looking in the mirror again."

Don't say it, Ellen thought. Don't mention the ghost in front of Agnes.

"There's Grandpa and Grandma," Ellen said. "Good-night, Agnes."

On the way home, Grandpa and Grandma told them about the new restaurant they'd been to and Corey told more Mighty Mike stories. When Grandma asked Ellen how her scene had gone, she said merely, "OK."

55

"Ellen's mad," Corey said. "She wanted to go early to look at the fairy dishes some more."

"After the haunted house ends and the museum officially opens," Grandma said, "we'll go some Saturday and spend as much time as you like."

"Thanks," Ellen said. Usually, Grandma knew just how to make her feel better. This time, she had mixed feelings. She did want to study the Wedgwood but she wanted to do it now, not some vague time in the future. Once the haunted house was over, she would not want to come back to Clayton House, even to see the Fairylustre.

Corey was more excited than usual on the way home because his teacher and some of his third grade classmates had come that night. Nicholas and his parents were there, too.

"I waved at Miss Thorson," Corey said, "just before I got my head chopped off."

ELLEN went right to bed. Most nights, she read for half an hour but that night she quit after only two pages, even though she was in a good part of her book. She didn't know why it was such hard work just to stand and pretend she was being burned alive, but she felt totally worn out.

The dream partially awakened her. As Ellen struggled to open her eyes, she was aware that she had dreamed of the ghost. Usually, Ellen had a hard time remembering her dreams. It always irritated her when Corey sat at the breakfast table and related a long and involved story that he said he had dreamed. She often wondered if his dreams were really so vivid that he could remember all the details, or whether he merely invented stories as he lay in bed at night and then, the next morning, he thought he had dreamed them.

This time, she knew she had dreamed and the dream was so realistic that she could not pry herself loose from it. In her sleep, she had grown suddenly cold. Now, in her half-sleep, she shivered and pulled the blankets tight under her chin. The cold continued. An icy fog surrounded her bed, swirling around her face and seeping down under the covers.

Ellen turned on her stomach and burrowed her face in her pillow but the bone-chilling air swept across the back of her neck. As she moved her head, trying to get away from it, she felt a hand on the back of her neck. The fingers lay like five slender icicles across her skin.

Ellen tried to open her eyes, wanting the dream to end, but her eyelids felt glued together. She was sinking, swirling, drowning in a sea of ice water. Her teeth chattered and she began to shake uncontrollably.

Someone moaned, a low, groaning whisper in her ear. "Ohhhh." The moan slowly formed a single word: "Ohh . . . end." The word was spoken laboriously, as if it were a great effort for the person to speak at all. When she heard the voice, Ellen was finally able to snap out of the sleep state.

She raised her head and blinked into the darkness, still shivering.

"Ooohhh . . . end," the voice said again, and Ellen realized that it hadn't been a dream at all. She rolled over, fully awake now, her eyes staring wide into the black bedroom. When she sat up, the cold hand slid from her neck to her shoulder. The icy air still surrounded her; the ghostly voice echoed loudly in her ears.

"Are you Lydia?" Ellen whispered.

Silence.

"What do you want?"

Silence.

"I don't know what you want. Why did you come here? Why are you haunting me?"

The hand left her shoulder. The cold air now seemed concentrated directly in front of her.

"Aaahhh . . . end."

End, what? Ellen wondered. End of me? End of my life? Was the ghost threatening her? Why?

Ellen forced herself to move. She lifted her hand out from under the covers and reached the lamp that sat beside her bed. As soon as she clicked it on, the voice stopped. The cold air vanished.

Ellen looked around her room. She saw nothing unusual. Her jeans and sweatshirt were still draped across the chair, where she had left them. Her poster of the Woodland Park Zoo hung on the wall next to the window. Her radio still sat on her desk; her library book lay on the floor beside the bed, where she had sleepily put it last night, just before she fell asleep.

And her bedroom door was still shut. Tight. The ghost had materialized in Ellen's bedroom without opening or closing the door.

End. End. What could "end" mean?

Even though she no longer felt the icy hand on her neck or the cold air around her, Ellen continued to shiver. It was partly from cold, partly from fear, and partly from relief that the ghost had left.

It was bad enough to see ghostly hands or an image in a mirror when she was at the Clayton mansion. It was far worse to have the ghost materialize in Ellen's bedroom, while she was sound asleep. For the first time in her life, Ellen felt unsafe in her own home.

The mansion was a spooky old house and even without all the sinister scenes being acted out, stories of Lydia's ghost had been reported there for years. But Ellen knew of no record of the ghost ever straying beyond the Clayton property.

As she lay there, trembling and wondering what to do about this strange midnight visitor, there was a soft knock on her door. Ellen tensed and clutched the blanket even tighter under her chin.

"Ellen? Are you awake?"

"Yes, Mom. Come in."

Her mother opened the door. "Is anything wrong? I got up to go to the bathroom and saw light under your door."

Ellen hesitated. Should she tell her mother about Lydia? She was tempted to pour out the whole story but she stopped herself. Not yet, she thought. Mom can't do anything to keep the ghost from coming, so why worry her?

"Nothing's wrong. I just couldn't sleep."

"Do you feel all right? You look pale." Mrs. Streater walked to the bed and put her hand on Ellen's forehead. "No fever," she said. "Your face is cool."

"I had a bad dream," Ellen said.

"Want to tell me about it?"

"I—I dreamed there was a ghost in my room. She touched my neck and she tried to tell me something but all I could make out was the word, 'end'."

It didn't seem quite so scary, now that she was telling Mom about it. Especially when she pretended that it had only been a dream.

"What did the ghost look like?"

"I couldn't see her. I just felt her hand and heard her voice. And I could feel cold air all around me."

"That's the funny thing about dreams," Mom said. "Even though you didn't *see* the ghost, you knew it was a woman. If it had really happened, you wouldn't know if it was a man or woman unless you saw the person."

Ellen didn't say she knew it was a woman because it was not her first encounter with the ghost. She didn't want to mention the ghost's reflection in a mirror.

"I've worried that this haunted house would give Corey nightmares," Mrs. Streater said. "Usually he's the one who has such realistic dreams. Maybe I should have worried about you instead. Not that my worrying ever makes any difference, anyway."

She patted Ellen's shoulder. "You don't have to finish at the haunted house, you know," she said. "If all those horrible scenes start to bother your sleep, I'll just tell Mrs. Whittacker that you can't do it any longer."

"Don't do that," Ellen said. "I want to finish." If she didn't, Grandma and Grandpa would be disappointed, to say nothing of Mrs. Whittacker. And Corey would be furious.

No, she would finish out the week. With the light on and Mom beside her, her courage returned. So did her curiosity. In spite of her fear, she was fascinated by the ghost, and puzzled. Why could she see Lydia and feel the ghost's presence when no one else could? Why did the ghost follow her home? What was Lydia trying to say, with her strange-sounding *ooohheenndd*?

Ellen was determined to find some answers and the place to do it was at the haunted house. She would manage to elude

Agnes and study the Wedgwood. One way or another, she would figure out what Lydia wanted her to see.

After Mrs. Streater left, Ellen turned off the light and lay still for a long time, unable to go back to sleep. She kept expecting the ghost to appear again.

When she finally fell asleep, she slept uneasily, waking often. The ghost did not return.

Chapter
8

T*rue Ghost Stories.*

The Streaters were browsing in a book store when Ellen saw the title in a special display of Halloween books. She opened it at random and began to read.

"Sometimes," she read, "a haunting is determined by what happened on the site years before." Like Lydia, she thought, who first appeared because Samuel's second wife tried to sell all the Wedgwood.

She continued to read, flipping from one chapter to the next and reading a sentence here, a paragraph there. When her parents were ready to pay for their purchase, Ellen asked if they would also buy the ghost book.

"Haven't you had enough of ghosts?" Mrs. Streater said. "I should think that is the last thing you would want to read right now."

Ellen was glad Mom didn't say anything about a bad dream.

"The book looks really good," Ellen said, "and I don't have anything to do when we get home." She had learned long ago that, while her parents usually said *no* to requests for new games or faddish clothes, they often said *yes* if she or Corey wanted to buy a book. It annoyed Corey, who could never sit still long enough to read more than a few pages, but even when Ellen was small, she had preferred book stores to toy stores. She had memorized the fairy books when she was three and then, with Grandma's help, she had learned to read before she started school. She still loved to read and often read her favorite books more than once.

When her parents looked uncertain about *True Ghost Stories*, Ellen added, "I suppose I can always watch television." Mrs. Streater agreed to buy the ghost book.

As soon as they got home, Ellen settled into a comfortable chair and, with great anticipation, began to read. She was glad the haunted house wasn't open on Sunday. The afternoon and evening stretched lazily before her like the first day of summer vacation.

Knowledge. The best way to fight fear is with knowledge. She had learned about Lydia Clayton's life from the biography. Now she would learn about ghosts. If she collected enough separate bits of knowledge maybe they would somehow fit together, like pieces of a puzzle.

She read straight through until dinner. The book was fascinating. Still, Ellen did not feel that she understood Lydia yet. Every ghost, it seems, is different and has its own reasons for doing what it does. She wished she knew what Lydia's reasons were.

After dinner, she stretched out on the sofa and kept reading.

"I'll say one thing for you," Mr. Streater remarked, "when we buy you a book, our money isn't wasted."

Ellen didn't hear him. She was reading a theory that some ghosts only appear at specific times of the year. One ghost always haunted a certain house at Christmastime. Another came only on the anniversary of a violent thunderstorm during which a favorite cocker spaniel was struck by lightning.

This wasn't true of Lydia, Ellen knew. According to the biography at the Historical Society library, Lydia had been seen in different seasons of the year.

The book said ghosts materialize most often in the dark but this didn't seem always true of Lydia, either. True, Lydia had disappeared from Ellen's room as soon as the light was turned on. But the dining room of the haunted house was lit when Ellen saw the hands and it wasn't dark when she saw Lydia's reflection in the mirror.

Ellen had nearly concluded that, while the book was interesting, it didn't pertain to her situation when she read about a man who sold his house and moved because he believed the house was haunted. He frequently heard footsteps in the night and claimed he could *smell* a ghost. He became so nervous he could not sleep and after months of restless nights, he moved.

On the first night in his new house, he heard the same rushing of footsteps which had become so familiar in the old house. He also smelled the distinctive odor of the ghost he thought he had left behind. After three months, he moved again and the story repeated itself. It became clear that it wasn't the houses that were haunted—it was the man himself. A ghost had attached itself to him and followed him wherever he went. Even moving to a different country failed to help.

Ellen quit reading and thought about that. What if the ghost of Lydia Clayton had decided to follow Ellen? Lydia had never left Clayton House before, or at least had never been seen away from it, until she appeared in Ellen's bedroom. What if Lydia kept haunting her? What if she continued to appear, night after night? Ellen shuddered, remembering how she felt as she was roused from a sound sleep by the cold fingers on her neck and the strangled sound of "Oohh . . . end."

She put the book aside and went to get a glass of milk and a cookie. Mr. Streater was in the kitchen making his lunch for work the next day. When he saw Ellen he said, "If you're interested in ghosts, why don't you look them up in our encyclopedia?"

"Good idea," Ellen said. She couldn't very well say that she had come to the kitchen to get away from ghost stories—not after begging her parents to buy her the book. Besides, her dad loved it when she and Corey used the encyclopedia. Whenever they asked him a question that he couldn't answer, he suggested that they look it up in the encyclopedia. Sometimes Ellen suspected he said that even when he knew the answer.

"Ghosts" were in Volume 13, which seemed appropriate. After a lengthy section on primitive religions, she read, "It is believed that certain people have psychic abilities which allow them to perceive that which other people do not sense, both in sight and hearing, just as some animals can see, hear or even smell that which humans cannot."

Ellen read that part again. Maybe this explained why she could see, feel, and hear the ghost even though no one else was able to. She thought back to the time when she knew, without being told, that Mrs. Lantow was sick. She had known about Uncle Ted and Aunt Cheryl's unhappiness.

Do I have special psychic ability? she wondered. The mention of animals who see and hear what humans can't made her remember how she had tried, last summer, to communicate with Prince as a Science Fair experiment. She had been successful in getting Prince to obey her unspoken commands. She had also communicated with an elephant at the zoo, although she couldn't prove that. Maybe she had unusual psychic powers. Maybe that's why Lydia had chosen her. Or maybe Lydia had no choice in the matter. Maybe Lydia was always there but Ellen was one of the rare people who could see her.

Knowledge. Ellen kept coming back to the idea that if she learned enough about ghosts, she would somehow be able to deal with Lydia. She finished her snack, put on her pajamas, and finished reading *True Ghost Stories* in bed.

It ended by saying that a person would learn far more about ghosts from just one personal encounter with one than by reading a hundred books on the subject. If that's true, Ellen thought, I'm already something of an expert.

That night, Lydia came again. Ellen woke shivering and knew, even before she heard the moan, that the ghost was back. She pulled the covers up over her face and squeezed her eyes shut tight. It didn't help. The icy air penetrated her blanket.

Ellen pretended not to notice. She lay still, hardly breathing. She heard a muffled, "Ooohhh . . . end," and did not respond.

Maybe if I ignore her, Ellen thought, she'll grow tired of bothering me and leave.

The mattress began to shake. It wasn't a gentle rocking movement, like the vibrating bed she and Corey had seen demonstrated at the county fair. It was instead a violent motion, as if a person stood at each corner of her bed and raised and lowered the mattress. At the same time, it tilted from side to side, until Ellen was afraid she would be flipped into the air like a pancake.

She clenched her teeth and clung to the bedding. The shaking grew more frenzied.

Ellen flung the blankets back, uncovering her face. "Stop it!" she said, trying to keep her voice low.

Immediately, the bed quit shaking.

"What do you want?" Ellen whispered.

The cold air that had pressed against her moved away. She felt it swirling a few feet in front of her, like a miniature tornado. Seconds later, the swirling stopped. The ghost appeared.

Ellen saw all of her. It was the same woman whose reflection Ellen had seen in the mirror. She wore the same long white gown, with lace at the wrists and throat.

"Lydia," Ellen said. It was a statement, not a question.

"Ooohhh . . . end." The ghost had a greenish glow to her, especially her huge eyes.

Frantically, Ellen tried to remember everything she had read about ghosts, wondering what she should say or do.

"Why have you come here?" Ellen said. She thought of turning on the light but her mother might notice and Ellen wanted answers, not more questions.

The ghost held up her hands and beckoned to Ellen.

"You want me to follow you?" Ellen said.

The ghost beckoned again.

Ellen shook her head, no. She felt safe in her bed, though she wasn't sure why, the way the bed had been lurching just then.

The ghost held out one hand to Ellen, as if urging her to take it and follow.

"No," Ellen said, but even as she spoke, she swung her legs over the side of the bed and sat up. Her feet found her slippers and slid into them.

Moving as if she were in a trance, Ellen took her bathrobe from the blanket chest at the foot of her bed and slipped her arms into it. She turned and faced the ghost.

She had to look up because the ghost was taller than Ellen. She saw the back of the ghost's head as it moved toward Ellen's bedroom door. When it reached the door, it disappeared.

I should get back in bed, Ellen thought. I should turn on the light. If Mom comes, I can say I wanted a drink of water. But her mind seemed to belong to one person and her body to another. Even as she told herself what to do, she did exactly the opposite.

Feeling as if she had been hypnotized, Ellen quietly turned the knob and eased the door open. She peered out. The ghost stood in the hallway, waiting for her.

It floated down the stairs. Ellen followed.

It flowed through the living room. Ellen followed, though she went around the furniture instead of moving through it as the ghost did.

The ghost went to the front door and disappeared. As Ellen approached the door, she heard the click-click of Prince's toenails coming toward her across the floor. She stopped.

Prince nudged Ellen with his muzzle, wanting to be scratched. The feel of his fur, the everyday gesture of rubbing his head, brought Ellen out of the dreamlike state she had been in. She stood there, quietly stroking Prince's fur.

Prince growled. The ghost reappeared on the inside of the door.

"Shush, Prince," Ellen whispered. "No bark."

Prince growled again.

The ghost did not appear to notice. She lifted her arms again and beckoned for Ellen to follow her.

Ellen shook her head. "I can't," she said. "I'm not allowed to leave the house at night, without telling my parents." It was true and, for once, Ellen was glad to abide by her parents' strict rules.

The ghost came closer. Prince bared his teeth and moved between Ellen and the door.

"What do you want?" Ellen whispered. "You can't expect me to follow you around in the middle of the night when I don't know what you want or where you're going."

The ghost's mouth opened and a low, strangled sound came out. Ellen sensed it was a supreme effort to speak, but the effort failed. The luminous green eyes looked so sad that Ellen expected to see tears flowing down the ghost's cheeks.

The whole room was filled with frigid air. The ghost lifted her arms and beckoned again, imploring Ellen to follow.

Prince growled.

Ellen's fingers closed around Prince's collar.

"Come, Prince," she said. She turned and fled across the living room, up the stairs, and back to her own room, with Prince beside her. She closed her bedroom door. "You can sleep in here tonight," she told Prince. She wondered if Prince had actually seen the ghost or if he had only sensed something was there.

She got back in bed and sat propped against two pillows, staring at the closed door.

I will probably never sleep again, she thought. I'll be too nervous about being awakened by a ghost. I'll die of lack of sleep, if I don't die of fright first. Or else I'll tell someone what's going on and get committed to a mental institution.

Why did I follow her downstairs? Ellen wondered. I should have stayed in bed. Does she have some power over me, to make me do what she wants me to do? Or was I still half-asleep until

Prince came along and brought me to my senses? What if Prince had not been there? Would I have followed Lydia? Followed her where?

Where had Lydia planned to go? To Clayton House? That was much too far for Ellen to walk, although perhaps a ghost had no sense of distance. Lydia just materialized wherever she wanted to be. Maybe she thought Ellen could do the same.

Too bad I can't, Ellen thought. If I could, I would materialize in the dining room of the mansion when Agnes isn't there and try to figure out if there's something about the Wedgwood collection that Lydia is trying to show me.

Eventually, Ellen dozed, awoke, dozed again, and finally fell asleep.

Lydia did not return.

Chapter
9

$\mathbf{A}$re ghosts logical? Ellen wondered. If they aren't, Lydia's strange behavior will never make sense, no matter how hard I try to explain it. If they are, then I must discover what Lydia is trying to tell me.

Ellen's head told her to stay out of the dining room. Her curiosity told her to examine the Wedgwood again.

The next night, Ellen and Corey got to the haunted house later than usual, arriving just in time to get to their places before the doors opened. As Ellen hurried through the great hall and up the stairs, she hoped Agnes wouldn't be annoyed with her for being so late. There had been an accident on the freeway and traffic was a mess.

When Ellen entered the parlor, Agnes wasn't waiting. Moments later, Mrs. Whittacker announced on the loudspeaker, "All actors in place, please. The doors will open in five minutes."

Since Agnes wasn't there, Ellen turned on the switches herself to start all of the special effects for the Joan of Arc scene.

Then she got on the platform and held her hands behind her, as if they were tied.

Mrs. Whittacker rushed into the room. "I nearly forgot!" she cried. "I'm supposed to get your scene ready tonight."

"Where's Agnes?"

"She's sick. She called this afternoon and I couldn't find anyone to replace her. We expect a small crowd tonight, since it's Monday, so I thought we could manage but someone from Sheltering Arms showed up to make a video and I had to show her around."

As she spoke she wound the rope around Ellen's knees and shoulders and tied her to the stake. "I see I didn't need to panic. I might have known you would start all your special effects without any help. You and Corey are wonderful."

Mrs. Whittacker hurried away just in time. The first visitors of the night entered the viewing space as Ellen closed her eyes and tried to look saintly.

As the fake crowd shouted, "Witch! Heretic!" and the real audience murmured their sympathy and fright, Ellen's excitement grew. She could inspect the Wedgwood tonight, to see if it held some clue to what Lydia wanted Ellen to know. She could go behind the rope and examine each piece as much as she wanted, without worrying that Agnes would find her and order her out of the dining room.

Mrs. Whittacker came promptly at ten to untie Ellen. As soon as she put her shoes on, Ellen hurried across the hall to the dining room. It was empty. She glanced in the mirror as she passed it and saw only her own reflection. Good. Maybe Agnes *and* Lydia would leave her alone long enough for her to get a good, close look at the Wedgwood collection.

Quickly, she crossed the room to the Wedgwood display and ducked underneath the rope. She had already decided that she would begin with the earliest pieces and examine each one in order. It had occurred to her that maybe Lydia was trying to get her to admire the older Wedgwood, the pieces Lydia herself had collected. Until now, Ellen had focused all her attention on the Fairylustre and perhaps Lydia didn't like that.

As she leaned toward a tea server from Lydia's original creamware set, she heard footsteps behind her. When she looked around, no one was there. Probably one of the actors rushing down the hall, she thought, eager to get home.

She turned back to the Wedgwood and heard the footsteps again. She remembered the man in the book, the one who had moved so many times but no matter where he went, he heard the same footsteps of a ghost. She realized that she, too, was hearing phantom footsteps, not real ones. Instead of looking behind her, she kept her eyes straight ahead, trying to concentrate on the dishes.

Seconds later, Lydia materialized. She looked exactly the way she had looked the night before, in the same long gown. She stood at the far end of the display, with her arms outstretched.

Instead of being scared this time, Ellen was annoyed. This was her only chance to look at the Wedgwood without having Agnes interrupt her. "What do you want?" she said.

"Oooohhh . . . end."

"I'm trying to figure out what you want," Ellen said crossly. "It would be easier if you quit popping up all the time and scaring me."

The ghost signaled for Ellen to come closer.

Ellen ignored her. She continued to look at the older dishes, one piece at a time. She didn't touch them because she was afraid she might accidentally drop one but she put her face only a foot or so away from each one and examined it carefully.

"Aaaahhend." The ghost motioned again, urging Ellen to the Fairylustre part of the display.

"Hey, Ellen. Are you ready to leave?"

She jumped at the sound of Corey's voice and then looked quickly toward the ghost. Lydia had vanished.

"I'll be there in a minute," Ellen said.

"Are you looking at those dumb old dishes again? I don't see what's so great about them. If you want to look at dishes, all you have to do is open the kitchen cupboards at home."

"The kitchen cupboards at home do not contain anything like this," Ellen said.

"I've figured out a way to earn some money so I can have a bike," Corey said.

"Oh?"

"I'm going to give screaming lessons."

Ellen rolled her eyes and did not answer.

"I'll bet there are lots of kids who would like to be able to scream as good as I do. Mighty Mike says I'm the best screamer he's ever heard, even counting people on TV. So I decided I could charge fifty cents apiece and teach all the other kids how to scream. Nicholas is my first student."

"Well, don't do it at our house," Ellen said. It was bad enough to hear Corey practice his screaming without listening to his friends, as well.

Ellen stood now in front of the Fairylustre. She had already studied it so many other times, she didn't think it was what Lydia wanted to show her, but she looked again anyway, just because she liked it.

"I can't decide if it should be private lessons or a whole bunch of kids at once," Corey said. "What do you think?"

"I think . . ." Ellen stopped. "Corey," she said. "Go get Mrs. Whittacker."

"You think Mrs. Whittacker would want to take screaming lessons?"

"Just do what I say. And tell her to hurry."

"I wasn't going to start the lessons tonight."

"Run!"

As Corey trotted out of the dining room, Ellen kept her eyes fixed on the bottom shelf of the Fairylustre display. Her heart quickened with excitement. This must be what Lydia had been trying to tell her. This was what the ghost wanted her to see.

In a few minutes, she heard Corey and Mrs. Whittacker returning. Corey was explaining how the screaming lessons would work.

As soon as Mrs. Whittacker was in the dining room, Ellen dared to take her eyes off the shelf and turn around.

"What is it?" Mrs. Whittacker said.

"A bowl is missing."

"What? Are you sure?"

"We've been robbed!" Corey yelled.

Ellen pointed to the bottom shelf. "One of the Fairylustre bowls is gone," she said. "It's always been there, on the bottom shelf. It's octagonal shaped and it has fairies and a bridge."

Mrs. Whittacker looked where Ellen was pointing. Her hands flew to her face and she drew in her breath sharply. "You're right," she said. "I know which bowl you mean."

"The purple people from Jupiter must have come," said Corey.

"It's the bowl I held that first night," Ellen said. "That's why I remembered it."

"Wow," said Corey. "How could they steal a bowl when there were so many people in here?"

"Not everybody who goes through the haunted house bothers to look at the museum displays in here," Ellen said. "Maybe one person was in here all alone and just went under the rope and helped themselves."

"Or maybe," said Corey, "it wasn't the purple people. Maybe it was a gang of thieves and they've had it planned for a long time. One of them pretended to be with the Historical Society and he told all the people that this room was closed tonight and then he stood guard while the other thieves went in and . . ."

"We mustn't jump to conclusions," Mrs. Whittacker said. "We don't know for sure that the bowl was stolen."

"It's gone, isn't it?" Corey said.

"I must call Agnes," Mrs. Whittacker said. She hurried through the upper kitchen to her office, with Ellen and Corey following her. Ellen knew her parents were probably waiting outside by now to take her and Corey home, but she didn't want to leave in the middle of a mystery.

As they entered Mrs. Whittacker's office, Ellen said, "Please don't tell Agnes that I'm the one who discovered that the bowl was stolen."

"Why not?" Corey said. "You're practically a detective. The police will interview you. You'll probably get your picture in the paper."

"I don't want my picture in the paper," Ellen said. "Not for this."

Mrs. Whittacker dialed the phone and waited. "Agnes? One

of the bowls is gone. The small octagonal Fairylustre; the one with the castle and bridge." She was quiet for a few moments, listening. Then she sighed, clearly relieved. "Oh, thank goodness," she said. "I was afraid someone had stolen it. I guess I forgot to tell you that we aren't supposed to remove it from the mansion. Yes. Yes, I can understand that. Well, I hope I didn't wake you; I realize it's late to call, especially when you aren't feeling well."

As Mrs. Whittacker continued to talk, Ellen quit listening, since the bowl was obviously safe. Instead, she thought about the ghost. Lydia must have wanted her to notice that the bowl was gone. That's why she motioned for Ellen to go to that end of the display. Maybe that's what she wanted last night, too, when she tried to get Ellen to follow her out the front door.

If that's so, Ellen thought, this might be the end of the haunting. I discovered the missing bowl, it's been accounted for, and all is well. Maybe I won't see Lydia anymore.

Relief flooded her. Even though she had stood up to Lydia earlier that night, she had secretly dreaded going to sleep again, for fear she would awaken to a cold wind on her face.

"What did she say?" Corey asked, as soon as Mrs. Whittacker hung up.

"She has it. She took it to her studio to repair a tiny chip on the inside of the rim. She took it home on Saturday, repaired it on Sunday, and planned to bring it back today. She hadn't thought to tell me, since she expected the piece to be back in place before I arrived tonight. When she got sick, of course, the bowl did not get returned."

"I didn't see a chip," Ellen said.

"Neither did I. That's why we're so fortunate to have Agnes. She notices everything, including the smallest flaws. And with her special training, she's able to do repairs even on old pieces. She restored a china bowl for me, one that belonged to my mother, and it's impossible to tell where she did it. The collection is in good hands."

"Rats," said Corey. "I was hoping it was stolen." Then, seeing the look on Mrs. Whittacker's face, he added, "I would want you to get it back and not have it be broken. But I thought the police might come and investigate. Maybe Ellen would have been a witness. Maybe she would have to go to court and tell how she knew that the bowl was gone and I would have to go, too, to tell how I ran and got you. Maybe . . ."

"Maybe you had better see if your parents are waiting for you," Mrs. Whittacker said.

They were. As usual, Corey ran ahead and began talking the minute he opened the car door. By the time Ellen reached the car, Mr. and Mrs. Streater had heard all about how Ellen and Corey had thought a bowl was stolen but it turned out that Agnes had taken it home to fix it.

Mrs. Whittacker walked out with Ellen and talked to Mr. and Mrs. Streater for a few moments. "I don't know how we would manage without these kids of yours," she said.

As the Streaters' car passed the gates at the end of the Clayton driveway, Ellen tuned out Corey's voice and thought about Lydia.

The first time Ellen felt the cold wind, she had been looking at the octagonal bowl. Agnes didn't take the bowl home until Saturday night. By then, Lydia had appeared to Ellen, one way or another, several times. If the fact that a bowl was missing wasn't what Lydia wanted her to notice, what was it? What did she want?

Ellen's anxiety quickly returned.

That night, Ellen awoke, feeling cold. The clock beside her bed said 2:30 A.M. For a moment, she feared Lydia was in her room again.

She lay quietly alert but did not see the ghost, nor did she feel a wind or the pressure of icicle fingers. Maybe I just got uncovered, Ellen thought. Maybe that's why I woke up.

She snuggled under her blankets and closed her eyes. Then she heard something. She raised her head, listening. The sound came again.

Prince was whining. He wasn't outside the door, trying to get in, as he sometimes did at night but she was sure she had heard him whine. He must have whined earlier, too; that must be what awoke her.

Prince never needed to go out during the night. Was he sick? Worried, Ellen swung her legs over the side of the bed. She put on her robe and opened her bedroom door. The whining came again.

She followed the sound into the living room and stopped. Lydia glided toward the front door. Although she was clearly visible, she was also transparent. Ellen saw Lydia and, at the same time, she saw her father's favorite reclining chair, which was directly behind the ghost.

Prince whined again and Ellen realized the ghost was not alone. As Lydia moved, Corey followed, a few steps behind her. Prince was next to Corey, pawing at the floor and whining, obviously trying to get Corey's attention.

"I'm not supposed to go anywhere without telling Mom or Dad first," Corey whispered.

Lydia moved ahead of him and beckoned for him to follow.

As Ellen watched them, she felt as if she were viewing a home video. She heard their voices and saw their actions but she did not feel like she was actually there in the living room with them. The scene had an other-worldly quality, a feeling of unreality, and she felt oddly detached from it. It was the same trancelike sensation she had experienced the night she almost followed Lydia out the door.

Corey stepped closer to Lydia. "If I go with you to Clayton House, will you come and visit my class at school?"

The ghost beckoned again.

"That would be so cool," Corey said. "If I tell Nicholas and the other kids I saw a ghost, they'll think I'm just making up a story. But if I bring you with me, they'll know it's all true."

Lydia floated through the front door.

Corey hesitated for only a moment. Then he said, "Wait for me," opened the door and went out. Prince tried to go with him, but Corey pushed the dog back, slipped through the opening, and shut the door.

As the door closed, Prince barked. Ellen's feeling of unreality vanished and she snapped into action. She dashed across the room, flung open the door, and rushed out. Prince ran ahead of her, barking frantically.

"Corey!" Ellen yelled. "Get back here!"

At the sound of Ellen's voice, Lydia looked back and raised her arms. Her entire body glowed with an eerie green light.

"Aahheenndd," she called.

Corey stopped walking. As Ellen approached him, she saw that her brother's eyes were closed. Was he walking in his sleep? He had talked to Lydia, as if he were fully alert. Yet, now he seemed like a zombie, the way Ellen had felt the first time, when she followed Lydia from her bedroom to the front door. She had felt that way again just now, watching Corey with Lydia. If the ghost had some power over Ellen, the power clearly worked on Corey, too.

Prince stood protectively between Lydia and the children. A low growl rumbled deep in his throat and the fur along the ridge of his back stood straight up.

Ellen gave Corey a gentle shove. "Get back in the house," she said.

"Aaa . . . end," Lydia implored. She motioned for Ellen to go with her. The glowing green eyes were enormous. They pleaded silently for Ellen to obey.

"No," Ellen said. "We cannot go with you. Corey is too young to follow you around the streets in the middle of the night. And so am I."

Ellen grabbed Corey's hand and pulled him toward the house. The porch light went on and Mr. Streater stepped out the door.

"What's going on?" he demanded.

Ellen blinked in the sudden light. Prince trotted toward Mr. Streater and Ellen knew without looking that Lydia was gone. "Corey was walking in his sleep," she said. "Prince woke me."

"We must have forgotten to put the chain lock on when we went to bed last night. Thank heaven you heard Prince."

Corey opened his eyes and looked around, as if wondering where he was.

"It's all right, son," Mr. Streater said. "You were walking in your sleep."

"No, I wasn't. I was following a ghost. She wanted me to go with her and then she was going to come to visit my school."

"You were dreaming," Mr. Streater said. "Prince heard you moving around and woke Ellen up."

"It was only a dream?" Corey sounded disappointed. "I thought the ghost was here."

Ellen knew it was better for Corey to think he had dreamed the whole episode. Otherwise, there was no telling what he would do in an effort to take Lydia to school with him. He'd probably sit up tomorrow night, waiting for Lydia to appear so he could leave with her.

When she was back in bed, Ellen lay awake for a long time. Why had Lydia chosen Corey this time? Had she given up haunting Ellen? Or had she hoped that if Corey followed her Ellen would, too?

Was Ellen wrong to let her father believe that Corey had dreamed about the ghost? If she told her parents what was really happening, what would they do? What could they do?

Ellen wished she had never agreed to help with the haunted house.

Chapter
10

Hey, Ellen!" Corey waved from the sidewalk. "We got a video of you on fire."

"Is it X-rated?" asked a voice from the back of the school bus.

Caitlin giggled but Ellen glared out the window. Moments earlier, she had been the center of attention as a group of boys who had gone through the haunted house asked her opinion about which scene was the fake one. Now Corey was spoiling it. She would have to ask her parents to keep Corey away from the bus stop until she was off the bus and it had left. The other kids must think she came from a family of circus freaks.

She stepped off the bus but before she could speak Corey said, "The video shows all the scenes from the haunted house. It has me screaming and you getting burned at the stake."

"Whose video is it?"

"Grandma brought it."

That surprised Ellen. Her grandparents had refused to come

to the haunted house because Grandma said she couldn't bear to watch Ellen and Corey in such dangerous situations, even when she knew they weren't real.

"Did Grandma and Grandpa look at the video?"

"Not yet. They're going to watch it with us. Grandma says she thinks she can stand to watch me get my head chopped off on screen if I'm sitting beside her, perfectly safe."

Ellen laughed.

"Maybe a Hollywood producer will see it and offer us movie contracts."

"I doubt that."

"Grandma said they might use part of it on TV on Halloween night, to advertise the haunted house. If they choose our scenes, a producer might see us. Mighty Mike's going to advertise us on the radio, too."

Despite her annoyance at her brother, Ellen walked faster. It would be fun to see a video of the haunted house, especially the Joan of Arc scene.

"Here are the stars of the show," Grandpa said, as Ellen and Corey got home.

"Where did you get the video?" Ellen asked.

"Mrs. Whittacker had a copy made for us. Someone from the staff of Sheltering Arms took it last night, so they can show it to Mr. Clayton, and Mrs. Whittacker thought we would enjoy having a copy to keep."

"Mr. Clayton?" Ellen said. "What Mr. Clayton?"

"Edward Clayton. The man who gave the mansion to the city."

"He's *alive*?" Ellen had assumed the mansion was willed to the city when the last of the Claytons died.

84

"He's in a nursing home, Sheltering Arms. He's quite old and unable to care for himself. He had private care at home for some years but he said he missed talking to people his own age so now he's at Sheltering Arms. The Director of the nursing home had the haunted house filmed for him."

"Let's look at the video," Corey said.

As scenes from the haunted house appeared on the television screen, Ellen's mind was in a whirl. It had not occurred to her that one of the Clayton family was still alive. She wondered if Lydia had ever appeared to him. Perhaps he knew things about the long ago hauntings—family stories that would not be in a published biography of Lydia.

Corey's bloodcurdling scream on the video brought Ellen's attention back to the screen.

"Good heavens," said Grandma.

"Rewind it," said Corey. "Let's play that part again."

Grandpa reversed the video and played Corey's part again. This time, everyone except Corey covered their ears.

Corey said, "Do it again."

"Later," Grandma said. "We want to see Ellen's part."

When the video showed King Haakon the Great of Norway being murdered by his soldiers in a pigsty, Corey declared, "That's the fake scene. What would a King be doing in a pigpen? Maybe I'll win the money."

"Mrs. Whittacker said the actors are not allowed to enter the drawing," Ellen said.

"I know," said Corey. "I tried. So I told Nicholas about the pigpen and he entered the drawing and if he wins, I get half."

"Shh," said Ellen. "Here's my part."

The screen now showed the village square and the distant

crowds. The shouting was clearly heard as the camera moved closer to Joan of Arc: "Witch! Heretic!" The flames leaped and hissed.

Grandma reached for Ellen's hand. "I'm not sure I can watch this," she said.

"Too bad they couldn't get the smoke smell on video," Ellen said. She felt like she was watching someone else, not herself. Joan had her eyes closed and her head back so her face tilted toward heaven. Her lips moved slightly, as if in silent prayer. People standing near the video camera could be heard saying things like, "Oh, that poor girl. Imagine what it would feel like."

Ellen blinked and leaned closer. A chill ran down the back of her neck. "Stop it for a minute," she said. "Please."

Grandpa hit the *pause* button.

Ellen stared at the screen. She saw herself, lashed to the stake, with the fake fire at her feet. And beside her on the platform, she saw Lydia.

"What are you looking at?" said Corey.

Ellen glanced at her grandparents and Corey. They were watching the same television screen she was. Didn't they see the ghost?

"Do you want to look at this part again?" Grandpa asked.

"No," said Ellen. "For a moment, I thought I saw someone else on the platform with me."

She held her breath while the others looked at the screen.

"Nobody there but Joan," said Corey.

"You probably got a glimpse of one of the painted figures in the backdrop," said Grandpa. "Do you want to see the rest now?"

Ellen nodded but she barely watched the rest of the video.

She had never sensed Lydia's presence during the Joan of Arc scene yet the ghost evidently had been there with her while the video was taken. How many other times was Lydia with her and she didn't know it? It was creepy enough to have a ghost appear out of nowhere; it was even creepier to think that the ghost was following her around when she wasn't aware of it.

Why couldn't anyone else see her? If the ghost got captured on film, then everyone who looked at the film should be able to see her. Yet, Ellen was the only one who did.

When the video ended, Grandpa and Grandma applauded.

Corey said, "Let's look at it again."

"We'll leave it here," Grandpa said. "Your parents will want to see it when they get home and you can look at it as much as you want."

"I'll fast-forward it to the part with me and Mighty Mike," Corey said. "Maybe I can use it to demonstrate when I give my screaming lessons."

Ellen saw Grandma and Grandpa exchange an amused glance but neither of them asked Corey what lessons he meant.

"Do you know if Mr. Clayton can have visitors?" Ellen asked.

"I could find out," Grandma said. "I have a friend at Sheltering Arms, recovering from a broken hip. I've been meaning to go and visit her."

"Maybe I could go with you," Ellen said, "and if Mr. Clayton can have visitors, I'll talk to him."

"That's a lovely idea," Grandma said. "So many patients in nursing homes never get visitors."

"Why don't you go now," Grandpa suggested. "I'll stay here with Corey."

Ellen and Grandma looked at each other and nodded agreement. Ellen was afraid Corey would want to go along, but he preferred to stay home and watch himself and Mighty Mike on video.

Ellen had never visited a nursing home so she wasn't sure what to expect. Sheltering Arms was spacious and bright, with bouquets of flowers in the lobby. Several elderly people in wheelchairs sat just outside the front door, enjoying the sunshine.

Grandma inquired at the desk and learned which room her friend was in. The nurse said that Mr. Clayton could have company. He was in Room 4, just down the hall.

Ellen hesitated in the doorway of Room 4. The door was open but the old man in the bed had his eyes closed. She didn't want to awaken him. As she wondered what to do, a nurse's aide bustled past. "Mr. Clayton," she called cheerfully, "you have a visitor."

The eyes opened at once and Mr. Clayton looked at Ellen. "Do I know you?" he asked.

"No," Ellen said.

"Good. I was afraid I was supposed to recognize you."

Ellen introduced herself and said she had a part in the haunted house.

He chuckled. "They showed me the movie," he said. "I hardly recognized the place. Looked like I hadn't hired a housekeeper in years." He squinted at Ellen. "Which part did you play?"

"I was Joan of Arc."

"Ah, yes. And a fine job you did of it." He motioned to the single straight chair in the room. "Have a seat. I'd offer you something to drink but this is the butler's day off." He laughed at his own joke and Ellen relaxed.

She looked around the small room. Mr. Clayton had a bed, a nightstand, and a small dresser with a television set on it. There were no rugs, no pictures on the walls. The spare furnishings were a sharp contrast to the elegant mansion.

"Do you miss your house?" she asked.

"No. It was too much for me. I loved it all my life but it is time to let someone else maintain it. Too bad I never married. Never had any children to pass it all on to."

"It was nice of you to give it to the city," Ellen said. "This way, lots of people will enjoy it."

"I hope so."

Ellen wondered how to approach the subject of Lydia.

"I can still go back, you know," Mr. Clayton said. "In my mind. I'm lucky that way. Some people my age have memory trouble but I can still go back and visit Clayton House, anytime I want. In my mind, I can wander from room to room and see all the furniture and remember the good times, when I was young."

"I like the Mexican silver fireplace," Ellen said.

Mr. Clayton smiled. "So many treasures," he said.

"I like the Fairylustre, too."

"Oh, the Fairylustre. That was always my favorite. In fact, I acquired most of the Fairylustre pieces."

"Tell me more about it," Ellen said.

"It's odd," Mr. Clayton said. "The appreciation of the Wedgwood seems to be something you are born with, like an ear for music. Certain people love it immediately; others are unimpressed with even the most beautiful pieces." Ellen thought of Corey.

"Neither of my parents particularly cared for it," Mr. Clayton went on. "As far as they were concerned, the Wedgwood was just some dusty old dishes that Great-grandmother Clayton had been fond of. But even as a small lad, I loved it. Too much, it seems, for I have the distinction of being the only person to break one of the original pieces. I was only three or four at the time but I can still remember the horrified reaction of my nanny when she discovered that, while she was chatting with one of the maids, I had removed a creamware plate and dropped it, smashing it into a dozen pieces. When I was older and my business was prospering, I sought out several fine old pieces. That's when I bought the Fairylustre."

"My favorite is an octagonal bowl," Ellen said. "It has a castle on it."

"I know which one you mean. I bought that for myself for my fortieth birthday present. More than forty years ago."

He laughed at Ellen's surprised expression. "When you don't have any family, sometimes you have to buy your own birthday present," he said.

"You picked a good one."

"Why did you come here? A pretty young girl must have plenty to do besides visit an old codger like me."

"I wanted to know more about your house and the Wedgwood. And . . ." She blurted it out before she lost her nerve: "I wondered if you know anything about the ghost."

"Ah. So that's it. The ghost stories are circulating again. I suppose that's to be expected when the whole building's been turned into a haunted house."

"I wondered if—if you ever saw her."

Mr. Clayton looked at Ellen so intently that Ellen dropped her eyes. When he spoke, his voice was barely a whisper. "You've seen her?"

Ellen nodded. "At least, I've seen some ghost and I think it's Lydia."

"When? What happened?"

It was a relief to talk about it. Once she began, the words came quickly, and the whole story poured out: the mirror, the floating hands, the night visits, and Ellen's belief that Lydia was trying to tell her something or show her something.

"I have the feeling she wants me to help her," Ellen said, "but I don't know what she needs or how I can help."

When she finished, Mr. Clayton said, "She isn't a bad ghost, you know. She's never hurt anyone. She only appears when something is wrong or when she's worried."

"Do you think she doesn't like the haunted house?"

"More likely, someone is disturbing the Wedgwood. My instructions to the city made it quite clear that the Wedgwood collection is to be displayed on the same dining-room shelves where it was when I moved out. The pieces are not to be moved."

"That's where it is," Ellen said, "in the dining room. They're going to install some brighter lights but the shelves aren't being changed."

"And no one is rearranging the Wedgwood or handling it?"

"Only Agnes."

"Who?"

"The curator of the museum. She's a potter, with her own gallery, and she's been doing some repair work on the Wedgwood."

Mr. Clayton frowned. "What kind of repair work?"

"She took home the little octagonal bowl that I like so much. It had a small chip and she fixed it."

Mr. Clayton's voice rose. "Someone chipped the Fairylustre? How? They aren't allowing the public to handle it, are they?"

"No. The area is roped off, to keep people back. I don't know how it got chipped. I only know that Agnes took it home to repair it."

Mr. Clayton thumped his fist on the bed. "When I turned that collection over to the Historical Society," he said, "it was in mint condition. If they're being careless with it, I may have to enforce my right to rescind the agreement."

Ellen licked her lips. She hadn't meant to stir up trouble or upset Mr. Clayton. She only wanted to learn about Lydia. "Did you ever see the ghost?" she asked.

"Twice. Both times when I was just a lad." He smiled, remembering. "The first time, I had picked some flowers in the garden and needed a vase to put them in. I went to the dining room and reached for the first piece of Wedgwood on the shelf. Instantly, I felt a chill and had the sensation of cold hands on my arm, restraining me. It frightened me so much, I ran out of the room and put my flowers in a glass jar from the kitchen."

"What happened the second time?"

"The second time, I was about ten years old. It had rained for a week and I was bored and irritable because I wanted to play outside. Having a somewhat active imagination, I decided to stir up some excitement by staging a robbery."

Ellen smiled. It sounded like the sort of scheme Corey would dream up.

"My plan was to hide some of the Wedgwood in my bedroom and then wait for someone, probably the downstairs maid, to notice that it was gone. Remembering how my nanny reacted to the broken plate, I thought the maid would scream and carry on hysterically and the whole household would come running. I put four or five pieces under my bed, after carefully wrapping them in bath towels. Nothing happened. The maid didn't notice they were missing. My parents didn't mention it." He shook his head. "Later, I wondered if they knew all along what I had done and had decided not to give me the satisfaction of reacting. At any rate, I slept that night with the Wedgwood under my bed and in the night, Lydia woke me. She grabbed me by the shoulders and shook me awake. I was so terrified, I couldn't scream. When she stood beside my bed and pointed to the floor, I knew what she wanted."

"What did you do?"

"I got up and returned all the Wedgwood to the proper place, right then, in the middle of the night, and I never touched it again. I never told my parents that I'd seen the ghost. They had always ridiculed the old ghost stories and I didn't want to confess what I'd done. That was the last time I ever saw the ghost. When I was older and found out how valuable the Wedgwood is, I decided the ghost was worried that I would be careless and break another piece. Later yet, when my father died and I learned about the baby's remains, I wondered if she was nervous that I would find them and dispose of them inappropriately."

"Remains?"

"Josiah's remains. Lydia could not bear to part with her baby, so she had the infant's body cremated and then put the cremated remains in a piece of her Wedgwood. Cremation was rare back then and Samuel told no one about this, fearing that Lydia would be considered insane. The secret was kept until his death; his Will divulged that Josiah's remains were in the oldest piece of Wedgwood, a black urn. He also stated that the Wedgwood collection must not be moved or sold. Those instructions have been honored by all of my family. When I wrote up my agreement with the city, I was quite specific about that."

"Maybe that's what Lydia is trying to tell me—that she doesn't want Josiah's remains disturbed."

"They won't be, as long as the Wedgwood is left where it belongs. I must say, I'm distressed to learn that this Agnes person took some of the Fairylustre home with her. Even though Josiah's remains are in a basalt urn, not the Fairylustre, my directions were for the entire collection."

He picked up a small tablet and pencil from the nightstand and wrote something down. "I have an appointment with my attorney tomorrow," he said. "I'll ask him to remind the City and the Historical Society of our agreement regarding the Wedgwood. They really must be more careful. Perhaps they'll need to post a guard, to be sure nothing else gets chipped."

When he finished writing, he winked at Ellen. "Should I tell my attorney that the ghost of Lydia is unhappy and causing trouble with Joan of Arc? Or do you think he'd assume I'm losing my mind?"

"It might be best not to mention Lydia." She felt more relaxed, hearing Mr. Clayton joke about the ghost. "I wonder, though, why me? Why can I see her and nobody else can? I haven't moved any of the Wedgwood. If she was trying to protect the urn, I should think she would appear to Agnes."

"Maybe she's tried."

Puzzled, Ellen waited for him to explain.

"There's an old saying from Confucius that goes, 'Everything has its beauty but not everyone sees it.' I think that's true of more than just beauty. The ghost might be there but only a person who is highly aware of feelings and vibrations will be able to see her. Some people are more psychically tuned in to the whole universe than ordinary people are."

Ellen thought of the other times when she had sensed, as Mr. Clayton put it, feelings and vibrations—situations that other people had not perceived. She could think of dozens of examples of times when she intuitively knew something that the people with her did not sense.

"Corey saw her, or seemed to," Ellen said, "when he was asleep."

"Perhaps in the sleep state, he was more receptive."

"Do you think she wanted to show Corey whatever it is she's been trying to show me?"

"Probably. Or perhaps she used your brother as a way to get you to go with her, hoping you would follow him."

"I almost did."

"I have a picture of her," Mr. Clayton said. "It was in a packet of old photographs that I found after my parents died. She's identified on the back as Lydia and I recognized her as the ghost who appeared the night I hid the Wedgwood under my bed."

"Is the picture here?" Ellen asked. "Could I see it?"

Mr. Clayton directed her to open the bottom drawer of his dresser and take out a small metal box. When she gave it to him, he opened it and looked through the contents for a minute. He selected a yellowed photograph and handed it to Ellen.

The smiling young woman in the picture held an infant. She looked so happy that for a moment it did not seem possible that she was the sad-eyed ghost. But the hair was the same and the face and—Ellen realized with a start—even the white night-gown with lace at the throat. Ellen turned the picture over. On the back it said, "Lydia and Josiah."

Ellen had felt all along that the apparition she saw was the ghost of Lydia Clayton. The picture proved she was right.

Grandma came to the door then and told Ellen it was time to leave. Ellen introduced her to Mr. Clayton.

"Thank you for coming," he told Ellen, as she put the metal box back in the drawer. "Except for my attorney, you're the first visitor I've had."

"Don't your friends ever come?"

He shook his head sadly. "That's the bad part about living to be eighty-one," he said. "Most of my friends have already died."

"I'll come again," Ellen promised. She liked hearing Mr. Clayton's stories of when he was young and it had felt good to talk about Lydia with someone who understood. Most of all it was a relief to know that he, too, had seen the ghost. Impulsively, she asked, "Do you want me to bring you anything next time?"

"Blueberry muffins." He answered so quickly that Ellen giggled. "The food here isn't bad," he explained, "but they never serve blueberry muffins. They were always my favorite."

"I'll make some myself," Ellen told him. "I can't come tomorrow, because tomorrow is Halloween and the haunted house opens early, but I'll try to come on Saturday."

"Next time, Ellen Streater," he said, "I'll know your name."

As Grandma drove Ellen home, she said, "All the money in the world and the only thing he wants is a blueberry muffin. How nice that you thought to ask him."

Ellen did not answer. She was planning what she would do at the haunted house that night. She would look inside the oldest piece of Wedgwood, the big black urn. She would see if the remains of Josiah Clayton had been disturbed.

Chapter
11

She wasn't afraid anymore. Mr. Clayton said Lydia had never hurt anyone and she believed him. Besides, the photograph of the happy young mother with her baby had made Ellen want to help the ghost if she could. She's a troubled spirit, Ellen decided, and for some reason she thinks I'm the one who can help her. Well, perhaps she's right; maybe I can help. I'm going to try.

Once, on a vacation, the Streaters had wandered through an old graveyard in a small town, reading the headstones. Ellen remembered asking her parents why so many of them said, *Rest in Peace*. Mom explained that many people believe unhappy souls become ghosts and wander the earth. Those who are happy have a peaceful eternal sleep.

Lydia was clearly an unhappy soul and Ellen wanted to help her. She felt sorry for anyone, even a ghost, who was in such anguish.

Besides, if she could solve Lydia's problem, whatever it was,

Lydia would quit haunting her. Even though she was no longer afraid of the ghost, she did not relish the idea of being awakened again in the middle of the night by an ice-cold hand on her neck. Or of always wondering if Lydia, unseen and unnoticed, was standing beside her.

All she had to do was figure out what Lydia wanted her to know. If the ghost was only worried about the remains in the urn, why did she urge Ellen toward the Fairylustre?

Lydia always repeated the same word, a moaning sound with "end" as the last syllable. Ellen started going through the alphabet, thinking of words that ended with end. Amend, attend, bend, blend, commend, defend, dividend, fend, friend.

She stopped. Could it be "friend?" Was Lydia trying to tell her that she meant no harm, that she was Ellen's friend?

She continued through the alphabet—intend, lend, mend, offend, pretend, recommend, send, spend, tend, trend, upend. None of the others made any sense in connection with the ghost. Friend did.

That night, Ellen walked through the great hall with a sense of anticipation. If Lydia appeared, she planned to ask her if that's what she meant. Surely the ghost would be able to give some sign if Ellen was right.

After she slipped into her Joan of Arc robe and removed her shoes and socks, she still had a few minutes to spare before it was time for Agnes to tie her, so she hurried into the dining room. The octagonal Fairylustre bowl was back in its usual place. Ellen ducked under the rope to get a closer look. She wondered if she might be able to see where Agnes had repaired the chip.

The bowl looked the same as it always had. Carefully, she picked it up, turning it around and around in her hands. She saw no hairline cracks nor any evidence of glue. She ran one finger around the rim of the bowl, feeling to see if it was smooth or uneven. She could detect no place that felt like a repair.

She turned the bowl again, to admire her favorite scene, and then stopped. The shoes of the fairy flying over the bridge were slightly different than they had been. Before, the toes of the shoes pointed up, with tiny gold balls on the tips. Now, one of the fairy's shoes went straight ahead, instead of up. Ellen examined the shoes carefully. The balls on the tips of the toes seemed slightly bigger, too.

How odd that Agnes would make such a change. Ellen wondered if she should say something about it. Probably Agnes would want to correct the mistake, if she knew. The whole point of restoration was to put a piece back exactly like it was originally.

She also wondered how the bowl got damaged. There wasn't any chip that first day, when Mrs. Whittacker showed her the Fairylustre. If there had been, surely one of them would have noticed it.

Ellen put the octagonal bowl back on the shelf. She would be glad when the new lights were installed. Even the shimmery Fairylustre seemed dull tonight, as if it needed to be dusted.

She went to the other end of the display, wondering if she dared peek inside the black urn to see if it contained fragments of human bones. As she approached the urn, Lydia appeared.

There were no preliminaries this time. No cold wind or running footsteps. No icy hands. She was just there, suddenly and completely. As usual, she motioned for Ellen to come closer.

"Ooohhh . . . end."

Behind her, through her, Ellen could see the shelves of Wedgwood.

Ellen spoke softly. "Lydia, are you trying to tell me that you want to be my friend?"

Lydia moved closer.

Ellen stayed where she was, hoping that she had guessed correctly about the word, *friend*.

"Ooohhend."

"Friend?" Ellen asked again, enunciating carefully: "You are my friend?"

The ghost stopped moving. The terrified expression in her eyes disappeared. "Foohhend," she whispered.

"Yes, I understand. You want to be my friend."

The ghost nodded her head.

"Friend," Ellen repeated.

The ghost quickly reached out and Ellen felt the cold hand on her arm.

Ellen gulped but did not flinch. "I want to be your friend," she said. "I'll help you, if I can."

Lydia spun Ellen around, pushing her back toward the Fairylustre.

"I saw the bowl," Ellen said. "I found the mistake Agnes made, when she repaired the chip. Is that what you're trying to show me?"

Lydia did not answer. She moved in front of Ellen, pulling her closer to the Fairylustre.

"I'll tell Agnes about the mistake," Ellen said. "I'm sure she'll be able to correct it."

Lydia tugged harder. Ellen sensed an urgency, as if the ghost feared that Ellen would not act quickly enough. Maybe, she thought, it isn't the repair job that's bothering Lydia. Maybe it's something more personal.

"I know about the black urn," Ellen said. "Mr. Clayton told me. Is that what's troubling you? Are you afraid someone will

100

disturb what's in it? Are you worried about your—about the remains of your baby's body?"

As soon as Ellen said *the remains of your baby's body*, Lydia screamed. It was not a low moan, like before, but a horrible, wrenching shriek, a blending of a woman's voice with some unearthly cry. It was a sound unlike anything Ellen had ever heard.

She jumped and felt gooseflesh rising all over her body. As the sound died away, Lydia disappeared. Realizing such a scream was sure to attract attention, Ellen quickly moved away from the shelves and back to the public viewing area. She couldn't let Agnes catch her examining the Wedgwood.

To Ellen's surprise, no one came into the dining room. She thought surely Corey would want to know who had uttered such a scream but neither her brother nor anyone else approached. Was Ellen the only person who had heard that awful cry?

It wasn't going to be easy to help Lydia. Ellen wasn't at all sure what to do next.

It was almost seven o'clock, so Ellen returned to the parlor to wait for Agnes. She wondered how to tell Agnes about her mistake on the Fairylustre bowl without making her angry. She supposed she could tell Mrs. Whittacker instead but that seemed like a mean trick on Agnes, since Mrs. Whittacker was Agnes's boss.

As it turned out, she didn't have a chance to tell Agnes anything before the haunted house opened. Agnes dashed in at one minute to seven, quickly tied Ellen to the stake, started the special effects and left again.

While she pretended to be Saint Joan, Ellen thought back over everything that had happened so far. Lydia seemed to want to show her something about the Fairylustre bowl but for the life of her, Ellen couldn't figure out what. It had not been the fact that the bowl was missing. Apparently, it was not the poor repair job, either. What, then? What did Lydia see that Ellen did not?

At ten, when the haunted house closed, Agnes failed to come and untie Ellen. She tried to wriggle loose but the rope was too tight. Fortunately, she spied Corey and Mighty Mike as they passed the doorway on their way out.

"Corey!" she called. "Agnes forgot to untie me."

Mighty Mike quickly loosened the knots and the rope fell to the ground. "Thanks," Ellen said. She bent down to put on her shoes and socks.

"I'll meet you downstairs," Corey said. "I want to walk with Mighty Mike."

"I'll be a couple of minutes," Ellen said. "I have to talk to Agnes." She had decided the best approach would be to tell Agnes privately about the mistake. That way, Agnes could correct it without embarrassment.

Ellen went through the doorway at the far end of the dining room and crossed the kitchen to the pantry which had been converted to an office for Mrs. Whittacker and Agnes. As she approached, she heard Agnes's voice. Ellen realized she was talking to someone.

The office door was partway open. Ellen peered in. Agnes sat behind the desk, smoking a cigarette, with her back to the door. "This is my last night," Agnes said. "No more Clayton House."

Ellen stopped. What did she mean? Was Agnes quitting?

"I had a bit of a scare last night," Agnes said. "Mrs. Whittacker noticed that one of the bowls was missing. I had taken it home with me on Saturday, after everyone left, because I couldn't tell from my photograph if I had done one of the fairies exactly right. Then I got sick and couldn't work on the bowl and couldn't return the original, either. Just my luck, she noticed it was missing and called me. I made up a story about repairing a chip and she bought it with no question. I never did get to compare the original bowl to mine."

Ellen's heart began to thud against her ribs. She couldn't see who Agnes was talking to.

"I've switched all but two pieces," Agnes continued, "and I'll do those two tonight, as soon as everyone's cleared out of here."

Agnes started to swivel around on the chair. Ellen flattened herself against the wall, behind the door, where Agnes couldn't see her.

Agnes kept talking. "Some of mine have been on the shelves for two weeks now and nobody can tell the difference. I told you I was good, Harry, and this proves it."

Ellen sidled away from the office door. She tiptoed back through the kitchen and into the dining room. She ducked under the rope and went straight toward the octagonal bowl. She picked it up and rubbed it carefully across her sleeve, to remove any dust. Then she looked at it closely.

It wasn't the lighting that made it seem duller tonight. It *was* duller. It was duller and the fairy's shoes were wrong and Ellen knew it was neither old nor valuable. She was not holding a piece of Wedgwood Fairylustre.

She was holding a fake.

Chapter
12

At last, Ellen knew what Lydia wanted her to see.

Why didn't I notice sooner? she wondered. How could I have been so dense?

She put the bowl back on the shelf and walked slowly past the other pieces. One of the Fairylustre vases didn't seem quite right to her, but she wasn't sure exactly why. She could not tell if the blue and white pieces were authentic or not. She couldn't tell the creamware, either, or any of the other pieces.

She stared for a long moment at the big black urn. Was it the same urn she had looked at that first day? Or was it a reproduction?

Even though she had studied the Wedgwood frequently in the last week, she could not tell which pieces were original and which were copies. Except for the Fairylustre bowl. That was a reproduction, for sure.

Agnes said she switched all but two pieces. If all of these

are imitations, Ellen thought, where are the originals? What has happened to the Wedgwood collection? Where are Josiah Clayton's remains?

Probably Lydia kept urging Ellen to look at the Fairylustre because that's what Ellen most admired. If she was going to realize a copy had been substituted for the real piece, it would most likely happen when she was looking at the Fairylustre.

Ellen felt stunned, short of breath, the way she had once when she was playing basketball and got the wind knocked out of her. She also felt angry. What right did Agnes have to steal these treasures? Ellen supposed Agnes planned to sell the real pieces. Maybe she already had. They might be gone, welcomed into private collections, anywhere in the world. They might never be recovered, might never again stand on the shelves of Clayton House.

Ellen thought of Mr. Clayton, lying in his bed at Sheltering Arms, giving his home and his treasured works of art to the city so that people like Ellen could enjoy them. How was he going to feel when he learned that the curator of the museum had stolen his beloved Wedgwood?

Well, she isn't going to get away with it, Ellen thought. Maybe the real pieces haven't been sold yet. Maybe there's still time to get them back.

She turned and ran across the dining room and down the stairs. She would tell her parents everything and they would call Mrs. Whittacker. Better yet, they could call the police. Maybe the police would come to Clayton House and catch Agnes yet tonight. She said she still had two pieces to switch.

Ellen rushed across the great hall. Corey was not standing by the door, where they usually met. No doubt he got tired of waiting for her and was already out in the car with whichever of their parents had come to pick them up, babbling about how good he had screamed tonight or telling yet another Mighty Mike tale.

She grabbed the door handle and pulled. Nothing happened. She pulled again. With a sinking feeling, Ellen realized the door was already locked. Mrs. Whittacker must have thought all the volunteers had left; she had gone out and locked the door behind her.

Ellen knew it took a key to unlock it, even from the inside. She did not like the idea of going back to the office and admitting to Agnes that she was locked in. She didn't particularly want to talk to Agnes at all—not until she'd been to the police with her discovery.

Before long, her parents would try to get in and would realize what had happened. But it might take a long time before they could reach Mrs. Whittacker or someone else who had a key.

Ellen would have to go and find Agnes, in order to get out. She went back upstairs and down the hall toward the dining room. Agnes was probably still in her office, talking to her friend.

As she walked, Ellen made up a story to explain why she had stayed in the mansion. She would tell Agnes that she thought Corey was still inside and she had gone to look for him. By the time she realized he had left without her, the door was locked. Unlike her brother, she was not used to making up stories but she certainly could not tell Agnes the real reason why she lingered so long after closing.

Her mind was on what she would say to Agnes as she entered the dining room and headed for the door to the kitchen.

She didn't see Agnes crouched beside the bottom shelf of Wedgwood.

Ellen was nearly to the kitchen door when she was hit by an icy blast of air so strong that she was forced to stop walking.

"Not now, Lydia," she said.

The moment she spoke, she heard a gasp behind her. Whirling around, she saw Agnes, still crouched beside the collection. On the floor beside her was a cardboard box. A piece of Fairy-lustre was in her hand. She stood up, quickly putting the Fairy-lustre on a shelf.

"Why are you still here?" Agnes said.

"I got locked in."

"What were you doing for so long?"

Ellen opened her mouth to give the story she had made up but before she could begin, Agnes said, "You were in here again, weren't you? You're the one who rearranged all the Wedgwood."

"No."

"I suppose you thought it was funny to put the newer pieces down at that end, where the dates are in the eighteen hundreds and put the old creamware up here."

"I didn't do that," Ellen said.

"I was in here personally while the public was here, to be sure that nobody got too close. The collection was in the proper sequence then. Someone rearranged it after the haunted house closed."

"It wasn't me."

"None of the other volunteers has shown any interest in the Wedgwood. Only you."

"I didn't move them around." She had to clamp her teeth tight together to keep from saying that Agnes was the one who had been messing with the Wedgwood, so why was she accusing Ellen?

"It won't do you any good to deny it," Agnes said. "I've already talked to Mrs. Whittacker about you. I caught her before she left and warned her that you can't be trusted to leave the collection alone and that she should watch you carefully until the haunted house closes, to be sure you stay away from it."

Ellen's mouth dropped open in astonishment. Then her eyes narrowed as she realized what Agnes had done. She wanted to be sure that nobody discovered that the real Wedgwood was missing. She wanted as much time as possible to get away, and she knew Ellen had examined the pieces thoroughly and might just notice that something wasn't right, so she made up a story about Ellen rearranging the Wedgwood, to be sure Mrs. Whittacker didn't allow Ellen to get too close to it.

Fury crackled through Ellen's veins. She was so angry, she wished she could point at Agnes and have bolts of lightning come out the ends of her fingers. She didn't even want Agnes to unlock the door for her. She just wanted to get away from that horrible woman.

"I'm going to call Mrs. Whittacker," she said, "and ask her to come and let me out." She turned and strode toward the kitchen door.

"Stay away from my office!" There was an undercurrent of panic in Agnes's voice.

Ellen kept walking.

Agnes started after her, tripped on the cardboard box, and fell against the shelves. Two vases toppled at the impact and smashed to the floor.

"Oh!" Ellen cried, as she looked at the shattered fragments. "Were they the real ones?" As soon as the words were out of her mouth, she realized what she had said. Her voice seemed to echo in the huge dining room. The real ones, the real ones.

"The real ones?" Agnes repeated. There was such animosity in her eyes that Ellen recoiled. They stared at each other for a moment.

"Harry!" Agnes shouted.

The kitchen door opened and a man wearing a blue ski parka ran into the dining room. He stopped when he saw Ellen. "Who's she?" he asked.

"She knows," Agnes said.

"What? You told this kid?"

"Of course not, you idiot. I don't know how she found out."

Ellen stepped backward, toward the dining-room entry.

"Now what do we do?" the man said.

"We'll have to take her with us."

"Oh, no. I'm not taking some kid across the state line."

Ellen tried to swallow but her throat was so tight, nothing moved.

"Do you have a better suggestion?" Agnes asked.

"We'll lock her in your office."

"With the telephone." Agnes looked disgusted.

"We can tie her up. Nobody will be back here until tomorrow afternoon. That's enough time for us."

"They'll come looking for her long before tomorrow afternoon," Agnes said. "They're probably trying to locate a key right now. We have to get moving, Harry. We're out of time. I'll get the last box; you get her in the car."

Ellen whirled and ran toward the door. The man's footsteps thumped on the floor behind her.

She ran into the hallway. He drew closer.

"There's no place to run," he called. "You're locked in here with us."

Straight ahead was the Joan of Arc room. Ellen knew there was no exit from that. To her right, the stairway led to the great hall and the front door; since it was locked, there was no point going that way. She ran to her left, toward the bedrooms. Bedroom doors sometimes lock from the inside.

She ran past the conservatory, where Corey and Mighty Mike did their scene every night, and past the library where the Julius Caesar scene took place. She saw a door ahead, a door that Mrs. Whittacker had not opened that first night, when she took them on a tour of the mansion.

She reached the door, turned the knob, and flung it open. It was not a bedroom. It was a linen closet. She whirled around and saw the man approaching, just a few yards away.

Ellen's mind raced, trying to decide what to do. She could try to run past him; maybe if she ducked, just as she got to him, she could elude his grasp. Or she could kick him. She could kick him in the groin and then run.

Ellen was not a fighter. She avoided conflict if she could and the thought of purposely kicking another person, with the intent of hurting him, was abhorrent to her. But it would be even worse to be forced into the car and be taken hostage by this man and Agnes.

There was no time to debate her options. The man lunged toward her. Ellen swung her foot toward him as hard as she could but he was too quick. It was as if he had anticipated what she would do and was ready for it.

As her foot lifted toward his groin, he clasped his hands together into a single fist and brought it down, hard, on Ellen's shin. The blow forced her foot away from him and, instead of

110

kicking the man, she kicked the wall. Ellen yelped as streamers of pain flew up her leg. She dropped to her knees.

The man unclasped his hands and reached for Ellen's shoulders.

Before he could grab her, the lights went out. The entire mansion was plunged into darkness. In front of her, Ellen heard the man curse.

Quickly, she rolled to her left and then crept away, moving forward, groping along the wall with her hand. She remembered that all the lights were on a timer. No doubt Agnes would have to go to some central control in order to turn them on again. That would take at least a couple of minutes—long enough for Ellen to hide, if she could just get away from the man now.

Behind her, she heard the man thumping the wall with his hands, as he tried to find her.

She crawled past the door to the library and the door to the conservatory. Hardly daring to breathe, she felt for the entry to the parlor. If she could get in there, she could hide under Joan of Arc's platform. She thought she could find her way to the platform, even in the dark. The man would not know where to look. If he found the door to the library, he would probably go in there, thinking she would enter the first room she came to. Even if he went in the parlor, he wouldn't be familiar with the Joan of Arc setup. He wouldn't know where to search.

If Agnes knew how to turn the lights back on, or got a flashlight, they still might not find her under Joan of Arc's platform.

Time, she knew, was on her side. By now, she was sure her parents were trying to get in. Maybe Mrs. Whittacker was already on her way back, with the key.

She crawled on. She must be near the entrance to the parlor.

A shuffling sound approached from her right. The man was moving down the center of the hallway, sliding his feet as if he were on skis. He was apparently trying to cover as much of the floor as possible without raising his feet.

Ellen scrunched tight against the wall, disappointed that the man had not gone into the library or the conservatory. The shuffling feet came closer. She held her breath.

The slight sliding sound of his shoes on the floor drew even and she was aware of his presence beside her. He passed her, moving slowly, as if he had his hands outstretched, trying to find her. Ellen remained on her hands and knees. After awhile, the man shouted for Agnes and Agnes yelled something in return.

Maybe they will decide to run for it, Ellen thought, and leave me here.

She found the parlor door and turned in, seeing the room in her mind and remembering how it was arranged. The public viewing area was first, then the thick velvet rope that kept viewers from going too close. She found one of the brass poles that held the rope and crawled past it.

There was a long expanse of floor next, made to look like a cobblestone street. Then would be the pile of sticks and branches, with the platform concealed on the backside.

She crawled faster now, eager to get under the platform. Her outstretched hand came to the brush pile. She crept around to the back. She felt the platform steps.

As she tried to move the sticks far enough away from the platform to allow herself to get underneath, the lights came on. Blinking in the sudden brightness, she yanked quickly at the platform, moving it just enough so she could squeeze through.

When she ducked down, her sweater snagged on one of the sticks. Tugging furiously, Ellen tried to disentangle herself. She heard footsteps running down the hallway toward her. This time, she knew it wasn't Lydia. These footsteps were real and they were far more dangerous than those of the ghost.

She jerked her arm, tearing the sweater.

"There she is!" cried Agnes.

Chapter
13

Ellen kicked and screamed. She clung to the wooden platform, getting splinters in the palms of her hands, but Harry and Agnes were too strong.

They dragged her away from the platform. Harry held her arms behind her back. "There's no way we can take her along," he said. "She'll slow us down too much."

"We'll tie her here," said Agnes, "to the stake." She grabbed the rope as Harry pushed Ellen up the platform steps and against the stake. He held her arms to her sides while Agnes wrapped the rope around and around, pulling it as tight as she could.

They wound more rope around Ellen's ankles and then around Ellen's waist. As Agnes reached around Ellen's face from behind to pull on the rope, Ellen bent her head and bit Agnes's hand as hard as she could. Agnes yelled and jerked her hand away.

The ropes cut into Ellen's skin. She knew there was no point trying to wiggle loose; she would only get rope burns.

"The last of the Wedgwood's in my car," Agnes said. "Bring the car around to the front and I'll meet you there."

Harry bolted out of the room. To Ellen's surprise, Agnes did not follow him. Instead, she waited until she was sure Harry was gone. Then Agnes turned back.

"Sorry, kid," she said. "But you should have minded your own business." She took a cigarette lighter out of her pocket. "I've worked for months on this job and I'm not letting you spoil it now."

She flicked the lighter twice. When a tiny flame appeared, she bent down, holding the lighter against the pile of sticks and brush at Ellen's feet.

Stunned by the realization of what Agnes was doing, Ellen stared silently.

"You've been practicing for this scene all week," Agnes said. "Now you can see what it's really like to burn at the stake."

Ellen screamed.

"There is no one to hear you." Agnes held the lighter steady against a twig. A tiny wisp of smoke curled upward toward the ceiling of the great mansion. In her mind, Ellen heard the sound effects from the Joan of Arc scene: the fire crackling, the shouts of the crowd. "Heretic!" "Witch!"

The twig caught. The bright yellow and blue flame stretched toward the other sticks. Ellen screamed again.

"A fire is a clever twist," Agnes said. "I wish I had thought of it sooner."

"You'll get caught," Ellen said.

"They won't be able to tell from the ruins that the charred vases and bowls weren't the real Wedgwood."

"My brother knows," Ellen said. "That's why I stayed here,

115

so I could detain you until he gets back with the police." In her panic, the lie rolled easily off her tongue.

"Corey doesn't know," Agnes said. "If you had both discovered that the Wedgwood was missing, you would both have run to tell someone."

More twigs caught fire. The smoke grew darker.

"They'll think we forgot to untie you," Agnes said, as she held her lighter to the other side of the brush pile. "They'll think something went wrong with this old, faulty wiring, and that you were not able to free yourself to escape the fire. It will be called a tragic accident."

A larger stick began burning. The flames spread outward.

Ellen closed her eyes. She couldn't bear to watch as the twigs and branches, one at a time, caught fire. Was it possible that her life would end like this? That she would never see her parents and Corey and Grandpa and Grandma again?

She shivered.

Her eyes flew open as she realized she had shivered because a strong icy wind was blowing at her back.

The wind surged past Ellen with such force that the heavy stake pushed against Ellen's back and she had to struggle to stay upright.

It blew across the platform, surrounding the pile of brush.

Agnes's head jerked up. "What the . . ?" she said.

The flames sputtered. The wind swooped back and forth, howling in its severity. The fire flickered, smoldered briefly, and then went out.

Quickly, Agnes tried to relight it.

The cold wind went mad. It swirled around Agnes, blowing her hair into her eyes. It lifted the smaller branches into the air so that they flew around Agnes, scratching her arms and face.

Desperately, she flicked the lighter again, but each time, as soon as the flame flared up, the wind blew it out.

"What's going on?" Agnes cried.

"It's the ghost," Ellen said. "I told you there was a ghost in here."

"That's nonsense. There are no ghosts." Agnes's hand shook as she frantically worked the lighter.

The wind centered itself beside her and blew with such force that the cigarette lighter fell from her fingers. It dropped into the pile of sticks.

"You've angered the ghost," Ellen said, "and now she's going to get you."

Agnes reached into the pile of brush, trying to retrieve the lighter. The wind became an indoor tornado, enclosing her. She abandoned the lighter and hunched over, shielding her face with her hands.

More of the smaller twigs and sticks were caught in the whirlwind and began blowing around and around Agnes.

"Harry!" she yelled. "Help!"

"He can't hear you," Ellen said. "He went for the car. No one can hear you except me and the ghost. And she is my friend."

"Make her stop!" Agnes cried.

Ellen said nothing.

Agnes twisted suddenly away from the pile of brush. She turned and ran toward the door but before she got there, the cold wind stopped, the swirling branches dropped to the floor, and Lydia materialized in the doorway.

The ghost looked much worse than the other times Ellen had seen her. For an instant, Ellen thought it was a different ghost altogether. The face was haggard, with sunken cheeks, and there were no eyeballs —just deep hollow, empty sockets. She

117

gave off a strong, putrid odor —like rotting meat that's been left in a warm garbage can.

But she wore the same lace-trimmed white gown, and the curly, shoulder-length hair was exactly like Lydia's. And then she made the same unearthly cry that she had made earlier, when Ellen asked her about the remains in the Wedgwood.

The ghastly cry was even louder than before and the high ceiling in the parlor made the horrible sound echo on and on. Ellen's pulse throbbed in her throat, in rhythm with the repulsive reverberation.

Ellen could not take her eyes from the apparition. Never had she seen anything so obnoxious. And yet, she felt no fear. She knew that Lydia was trying to help her. If the ghost had not intervened, the entire pile of brush would be burning by now, and Ellen with it.

"Aaaeeeiiigghhh!" As she cried this time, Lydia lifted her arms, as if to enfold Agnes and draw her close.

Agnes grabbed a large branch from the pile of sticks and lunged at the ghost. Gripping the limb with both hands, Agnes held it shoulder high and aimed it directly at Lydia's head.

The branch passed easily through Lydia's body. As it did, she made a low, guttural sound, like a wild animal growling.

Agnes opened her mouth but no sound came out. She dropped the branch. She backed away from Lydia.

Lydia raised her hands and reached for Agnes's throat.

As the ice-cold hands touched Agnes's skin, she fainted, falling in a heap just inside the doorway.

The ugly, foul-smelling apparition instantly vanished. In its place, stood the same sad young woman that Ellen had always seen before.

Downstairs, voices called, "Ellen? Are you in here?"

"Up here!" she shouted. "In the parlor!"

Lydia disappeared.

Footsteps thundered up the stairs.

"In here," Ellen cried again.

She expected to see Mrs. Whittacker. Instead it was a police officer, followed closely by Corey.

"I told you she was in trouble," Corey said. "A flying saucer could land on that little balcony and purple people from Jupiter might try to kidnap Ellen." Seeing the inert Agnes on the floor, he knelt beside her. "The purple people from Jupiter have killed Agnes!" he yelled.

Even with his mouth going as usual, Ellen was glad to see her brother. Her parents were right behind Corey.

"She isn't dead," Ellen said. "But she tried to kill me. She stole all the Wedgwood and put fake pieces on the shelves and when I found out, she tried to set fire to Clayton House."

"We realized you were locked in," Mrs. Streater said, "and we couldn't reach Mrs. Whittacker, so we called the police."

The officer began to untie Ellen. "When we arrived," he said, "we found a man sitting out in front in a car, with the engine running."

"That's Harry," Ellen said. "He and Agnes tied me up."

Agnes groaned and sat up. She looked at the police officer and groaned again.

"How did you knock Agnes out, when she had you tied up?" Corey asked.

"I didn't. She fainted." Ellen looked at Agnes, wondering if Agnes would say anything about the ghost.

"I didn't faint," Agnes said. "I slipped and hit my head on the floor."

"No," said Ellen. "She saw the ghost of Lydia Clayton, and

she fainted." She rubbed her arms, where the rope had cut into them.

The police officer raised his eyebrows and looked at her.

"Somehow, everyone forgot to untie Ellen tonight," Agnes said. "I was just leaving, when I heard her call. I came up to untie her but I tripped on one of these branches. I must have knocked myself out when I fell."

"Agnes tried to start a fire," Ellen said. "She and Harry tied me here and then she was going to burn Clayton House and me with it. The twigs were already starting to burn when Lydia's ghost blew out the flame."

"That's ridiculous," Agnes said. "Why would I burn down my place of employment? *I* wouldn't collect any insurance. And there certainly was no ghost involved."

"Are you sure it wasn't purple people from Jupiter?" Corey said.

"Just like my kids," said the police officer to Mr. and Mrs. Streater. "Terrific imaginations."

Mr. and Mrs. Streater looked at each other, as if wondering what to believe.

"It wasn't my imagination," Ellen said. "I've seen the ghost before. The other times, I was the only one who could see her but this time, Agnes saw her, too."

"Ellen doesn't normally make up stories," Mr. Streater said.

"I do seem to smell smoke," Mrs. Streater said.

"Mighty Mike and I untied Ellen," Corey said. "Before we left, we came in here and Mighty Mike untied the rope."

"Mighty Mike McGarven?" said the officer. "The D.J.?"

"You can call him and ask him," Corey said. "He'll remember."

"There's where the fire was," Ellen said. She pointed to the charred black places where the twigs had started to burn.

The officer bent to look more closely. "There's the cigarette lighter," he said, reaching into the pile of wood and picking Agnes's lighter off the floor.

"Did you scream?" asked Corey.

"Yes."

"Good." Corey smiled in satisfaction. "She learned how from me," he said, but the police officer was no longer listening to Ellen and Corey. He was busy telling Agnes her rights.

"You could have been killed," Mrs. Streater said, as she hugged Ellen.

"And this beautiful mansion might have burned to the ground," said Mr. Streater.

"Did you really see the ghost?" asked Corey.

"Yes."

"Did you ask her about visiting my class at school?"

Ellen gave him a disgusted look. "I had a few other things on my mind," she said.

"Well, if you see her again, be sure to ask."

A second officer arrived. "I didn't find any drugs or weapons on the guy," he reported, "but another squad car took him for questioning. There are several boxes of old dishes in the car that look like they might be valuable."

"The Wedgwood!" all the Streaters said, together.

"And he had two plane tickets for London in his pocket, leaving at midnight tonight."

"Looks like you'll miss your flight," the first officer said to Agnes, as he snapped handcuffs on her and led her away.

The other officer questioned Ellen awhile longer and then thanked her and told the Streaters they could go.

"But you didn't call the newspaper," Corey said. "Aren't you going to call the newspaper and have someone come and take our picture?"

"Not this time," said Mr. Streater.

"We could wait awhile," Corey said, "until they get here."

"This family," said Mrs. Streater, "will be the death of me."

Chapter
14

Those were the best blueberry muffins I ever ate," Mr. Clayton said. "How you had time to make them with all the goings on last night, I'll never know."

"I stayed home from school today," Ellen admitted. "I was worn out."

"Small wonder. I heard the news story about you this morning. How you caught that Agnes person and her partner."

"Not the whole story."

"Oh?"

"Lydia saved my life—and she saved Clayton House from burning. But Agnes denied seeing the ghost and the police officer thought I was making that part of the story up."

"Why would you do that? You told the truth about everything else, didn't you?"

"Of course. I wouldn't lie to the police. But apparently Corey had been bombarding them with his outlandish theory that I was kidnapped by purple people from Jupiter, so when I started talking about a ghost, the officer ignored me, too. It was the best part of the whole episode and he didn't believe me."

"So tell me. I'll believe you."

Ellen smiled at him and told him everything, exactly as it had happened. "She looked horrible, much worse than the other times."

"Maybe a ghost appears one way to her friends and another way to her enemies."

"I'll never be afraid of her again," Ellen said, "no matter how she looks. If she hadn't blown out the fire, I would not be here today, talking to you."

Mr. Clayton shook his head. "It's hard to believe that anyone would set fire to Clayton House, let alone try to murder you."

"Agnes was in big financial trouble. Mrs. Whittacker found out this morning that Agnes owed a huge amount in back rent for her gallery and had other debts, as well. She and Harry had already shipped all of Agnes's gallery pieces to London and had rented shop space there."

"No doubt they planned to sell the stolen Wedgwood."

"Mrs. Whittacker says they'd have no trouble finding buyers."

"So Lydia saved your life." Mr. Clayton nodded his head, looking satisfied. "I always did think she was a kindly ghost, not at all like the stereotype that everyone fears."

"The police called my house this morning. They had a list of the Wedgwood from the Historical Society and they found all the missing pieces in Agnes's car."

"What about the pieces that broke, when Agnes fell?"

"They were fakes that Agnes had made."

"Thank heaven."

"As we were leaving Clayton House last night," Ellen said, "I pretended I'd forgotten my jacket and ran back upstairs alone. I was hoping I could see Lydia and thank her, but she wasn't there."

"You may never see her again. She doesn't need you anymore, now that they've recovered all the Wedgwood, unharmed."

"It would be a relief not to be haunted anymore but I would like a chance to tell Lydia how grateful I am."

"I imagine she knows that, without being told."

"When Mrs. Whittacker came over this morning, she said that Josiah's remains were still in the urn. She knew about them and had been worried, too. She said to tell you, all of the Wedgwood is back on the shelves in their original places and they won't be moved again."

"One piece will be," Mr. Clayton said.

"I don't think so," Ellen replied. "Mrs. Whittacker seemed determined to make sure that nothing like this happens again."

"*I'm* removing one piece," Mr. Clayton said. "The octagonal Fairylustre bowl. I told my lawyer this morning to withdraw it from the list of pieces that I'm giving to the city."

"I don't understand." Ellen looked at the small dresser top, already crowded with Mr. Clayton's television, a box of tissues, and some shaving equipment. "Aren't you afraid it will get broken, if you keep it here?"

"I don't plan to keep it here. It's yours."

Ellen stared at him.

"If it hadn't been for you, the entire collection would have been lost. The little bowl seems like a fitting reward."

"I don't need a reward," Ellen said. "Besides, Lydia is the one who should be thanked."

Mr. Clayton chuckled. "Lydia got what she wanted," he said. "It pleases me to give the little bowl to someone who appreciates it and will love it as much as I always have."

"Thank you," Ellen said. "I'll treasure it always." Her smile faded. "But Lydia might not like it if I take the Fairylustre bowl. What if she keeps haunting me?" Even though Ellen was no longer afraid of Lydia, she did not relish the idea of being awakened in the night by cold hands on her face.

"Lydia has appeared only when the Wedgwood was in danger. She first came back, years ago, when Caroline Clayton kept trying to get rid of the Wedgwood. As a small boy, I was clearly a threat."

"The first time I felt the ghost was when Mrs. Whittacker handed the Fairylustre bowl to Corey."

"Exactly. Another small, and probably careless, boy. I believe Lydia was determined that the Wedgwood not be harmed and her baby's remains not be disturbed. Since you are the one who prevented that from happening, she should be happy to see you rewarded. And I know you would be careful with the bowl."

"If Lydia appears tonight at the haunted house, I'll tell her about your gift and ask her if she'd object."

"I don't think you'll see Lydia again. I think the ghost appeared only because the Wedgwood was being stolen and the black urn removed from Clayton House. Now that the whole collection is safe, there's no reason for her to be restless."

To her own surprise, the idea of never seeing Lydia again disappointed Ellen. When she thought about that, she realized she had been hoping she would see the ghost once more, but this time looking happy, the way the smiling Lydia looked in Mr. Clayton's old picture as she cuddled her precious baby.

126

As she thought of the picture, a new idea hit Ellen. "I wonder," she said.

"Yes?"

"I wonder if what she really wants is to be near her baby."

Mr. Clayton looked startled. "What do you mean?"

"The biography of Lydia said she became a recluse after Josiah died, spending all of her time with her Wedgwood, but the biographer didn't know about the baby's remains. Maybe Lydia was really only trying to stay close to all she had left of Josiah. Maybe she *still* wants that. I saw her hands come out of the black urn."

Mr. Clayton looked thoughtful. "Perhaps Samuel had the same idea. Maybe that's why he suggested digging up Lydia's coffin, cremating her body, and putting her remains in the Wedgwood. He might have guessed how Lydia felt."

"But Caroline wouldn't let him do it," Ellen said.

"And he couldn't tell Caroline his real reason because she didn't know about Josiah's remains."

"Maybe it isn't the Wedgwood Lydia cares about; it's Josiah."

Mr. Clayton nodded. "I think you're right. All these years, she's been trying to tell someone to bury her baby's remains where she is buried, so they can be together. How did you think of this?"

"Lydia looked so happy in your picture and she looks so sad now. I just tried to figure out what would make her happy again."

"I'll have it done immediately. Lydia's buried in the Clayton family plot so it will be no problem and this will insure that Josiah's remains are never disturbed in the future. I should have thought of this long ago."

127

"Perhaps it's just as well you didn't have Josiah's remains buried sooner. Lydia may not care about the Wedgwood, once her baby's remains are no longer in the urn, and if Lydia had not appeared, Agnes would have succeeded in stealing the Wedgwood."

Grandma entered Mr. Clayton's room. "Are you ready to leave?" she asked Ellen. "It's Halloween, you know. I have to buy goodies in case anyone comes for trick or treat. I don't dare buy candy bars ahead of time, or Grandpa eats them."

Ellen took Mr. Clayton's hand. "Thank you again. It's the best present I ever got."

Looking serious, he shook a finger at Ellen. "There's one string attached," he warned. "You must bring blueberry muffins again."

"I'll come every Saturday."

HALLOWEEN. The final night of the haunted house. Ellen wondered if she would see the ghost one last time.

At home, Mrs. Streater said, "Corey went to a Halloween party at Nicholas's house and he isn't back yet. You won't need to leave for another hour."

"In that case," Ellen said, "I'm going to take a nap."

Ellen rarely slept in the daytime but the stress and excitement of the last few days had worn her out and with Corey gone, the house was quiet, for a change.

She turned on her radio, stretched out on her bed, and closed her eyes. The music soothed her and she felt her muscles relax. For the first time in several days, she fell asleep without worrying that she would be awakened by a ghost.

When the song ended, a shrill, fearsome scream jolted Ellen's nerves. She gasped and raised her head from the pillow, scanning the room. For an instant, she thought Lydia was back and that something else was wrong. Then she heard Mighty Mike say, "The scream you just heard was Prince Rufus; he will get beheaded tonight, beginning at . . ." Realizing it was a promotional spot for the haunted house, Ellen reached for the radio knob and switched it off.

There is no escaping my brother's voice, she thought. Even when he isn't here, I have to listen to him scream.

AS ELLEN stood tied to the stake that night, the sound effects of the crackling fire seemed more frightening than ever. The bright, artificial flames looked real as they flickered upward and the smoke smell stung her nostrils. When she looked down at the pile of brush and twigs, she saw blackened ones and knew they had been charred the night before.

I came so close, Ellen thought, and she was flooded with gratitude. Without Lydia, the experience of being burned alive would have been a horrible reality.

There was a huge crowd that night and many more people than usual took time to admire the Wedgwood collection. A beaming Mrs. Whittacker declared that Ellen's brush with danger and Agnes's arrest had certainly resulted in some fine publicity. People who ordinarily would have ignored the Wedgwood collection now stood in line to see the dishes that were so old and valuable a respected artist had ruined her career by replacing the real pieces with replicas.

"Ticket sales surpassed our goal by 20 percent," Mrs. Whittacker said. "We have enough money to replace the wiring, renovate the kitchen, and have some left over for future improvements."

Ellen decided it was just as well the newspapers and television stations did not know about Lydia. If they had broadcast news of a brave ghost who put out a fire, stopped a fleeing thief, and prevented a murder, Clayton House would be so jammed with gawkers that the haunted house would never be able to function.

Shortly after midnight, Ellen removed the Joan of Arc gown for the last time and joined the crowd who had gathered in the great hall to watch Mrs. Whittacker draw the winning name from those who correctly guessed which scene was not factual. Corey and Mighty Mike were already there and Ellen saw Corey wriggling with impatience as he waited to see if Nicholas's name was selected.

Mrs. Whittacker quieted the group by holding up a large glass bowl filled with slips of paper. "As you can see," she said "many people correctly guessed that the fictional scene was the one in the conservatory. No Prince Rufus was beheaded at the age of ten."

"*I* was the fake?" Corey's horrified voice rang out. "*I* was the fake and the pigs were real?"

As Mighty Mike consoled Corey and Mrs. Whittacker reached into the bowl for the winning name, Ellen slipped away. She went back upstairs and into the dining room.

She looked at the beautiful little Fairylustre bowl, its shimmery colors gleaming. As she thought of all the people who must have admired it that night, she decided to leave it where it was. It belonged to her and she would treasure that knowledge, but she wanted to have it displayed with the rest of the Wedgwood, where other people could enjoy it, too.

She held the bowl for a moment, turning it slowly. It was still hard to believe that anything so beautiful was hers. The thought made her glow with pleasure.

I'll have a little plaque made, she decided, a small brass plaque that says: *This piece is on loan from Ellen Streater*. I'll leave my Fairylustre bowl here in Clayton House, with the rest of the Wedgwood. She felt Lydia would approve of her decision.

Ellen walked to the other end of the display and stood in front of the oldest piece of Wedgwood, the black urn which contained the cremated remains of Josiah Clayton.

Did Lydia already know of Mr. Clayton's plan to bury Josiah's remains for all eternity beside his loving mother? Had she been present, unseen, at Sheltering Arms when Ellen wondered if the hauntings were motivated not by greed over her Wedgwood collection but by Lydia's love for her child?

"Lydia?" she whispered. "Are you here?"

Silence.

"Can you hear me, Lydia? If you can, please give me a sign."

Nothing. There was no cold air, no breeze, no hint that anyone other than Ellen was in the dining room. Ellen looked over her shoulder, toward the mirror. She saw only her own reflection.

"Lydia?" She said it louder this time, even though she knew that if the ghost were present, she would hear Ellen's voice at any sound level.

Silence.

Ellen waited a moment before she spoke again. "I want to

131

thank you, Lydia. You saved my life and I will always remember you."

Nothing. No hands, no face in the mirror, no chill.

Ellen stood quietly for a few more minutes. As she gazed at the shelves of Wedgwood, she realized that all the feelings of apprehension that she'd had about the house initially were gone. There was no more tension in the air, no coldness. The sinister vibrations which had disturbed her on her first visit were no longer here. Clayton House felt serene.

Ellen laid her fingers on the old black urn. Lightly, she caressed the piece which contained the last remains of Lydia Clayton's baby. As her hands moved slowly across the surface, she knew Mr. Clayton was right. She would not see Lydia's ghost again. She could only hope that her words of thanks, or her thoughts, were somehow perceived by the ghost.

Ellen smiled at the old Wedgwood urn.

"Rest in peace," she said softly. "Rest in peace, my friend."

About the Author

Peg Kehret lives with her husband, Carl, and their animal friends in an old farmhouse in Washington State. They have two grown children and four grandchildren. They enjoy traveling throughout the U.S., where Peg speaks at schools, sharing her enthusiasm for books and writing.

Peg's popular novels for young people frequently appear in awards lists. Her Minstrel titles include *Horror at the Haunted House*; *Nightmare Mountain* (Nebraska Golden Source Award; Young Hoosier Book Award; West Virginia Children's Book Award Honor Book; International Reading Association Children's Book Council Children's Choice); *Sisters, Long Ago* (International Reading Association Young Adults' Choice); *Cages* (an ALA Recommended Book for Reluctant Readers; International Reading Association Young Adults' Choice); *Terror at the Zoo,* and her forthcoming series, *Frightmares*.